[JYZEBURST]

Annals of The Jyze Age

Jyzeburst

Jyzemelt

Jyze and Jyze Alone

Jyze in Love

Deep Jyze

The Jyze Millennium

Jyze of the Heavenly Year

Scat Jyze

Jyzeburst

G.P. Sandefjord

Annal One of The Jyze Age

Cover art by GPS
Published by House of Jyze
ISBN 978-0-9964173-1-0
Library of Congress CIP pending
www.HouseOfJyze.com

To Lady U

    Jyze is neither politics nor
philosophy. Jyze is jyze, and
one's objective as a jyzer is to
achieve jyze.

                    -- Wallace Stevens
                    [but he said "poetry"
                    for "jyze" and "poet"
                    for "jyzer"]

BOOK I

CHAPTER ONE

[The Origin of Jyze]

1.

     Sunlight streaming in over my left shoulder. Birds
chirping. Dewdrops glittering in the grass and
windowfuls of leaves holding stock still. Incandescent
green. Forest green. (So many greens!)
     And this armchair is green. Threadbare chartreuse/
pea green (ugh) but comfortable. Not for a number of
years have I done any serious scratching in it and so
this is exciting. Or that's one of the reasons.
     Hold on.
                              *
     Just donned the "DREAM" cap. It was hanging on a
nail up there. It's colorful patchwork on a black
background with the word "DREAM" inscribed on the brim
in antically jumbled block capital letters. Just the
sort of corny thing fictive Mom might've sent fictive
son G back in the day. "Hang on to your dreams, kid."
Except she wouldn't say "kid"; she'd say "darling."
(Fictive Dad would smile, maybe, and roll his eyes.)
     -- Leaky No. 3 is giving me lots of grief right
now. Could be going at it with the comp book canted
oddly on my knee is why. Have to stop every few words
-- then happen upon a long flowing stretch, maybe as
many as thirty words, as with (oops) (as with this
sequence right here, wanted to say: excellent timing).
-- Where the sentences get jerky, confused, telegraphic,
it's No. 3's doing. Swear to god.
     Whole-wheat fig bars. Caramel ice cream, a

lingering taste slowly turning sour on my coated tongue.
    Soon a whole stable of X-BBs, each of which will
stroke like a dream. "In dreams begin responsi" -- aw
not that! Not now!
    The underside of the colorful brim is hanging down
into my upper peripheral vision like a gaudy theater
marquee on opening night. Reminding me of many a brim
gone by and many an opening night too, not to mention a
closing here and there. Beneath all those brims,
though, or at least the ones of my adult years, say,
when it counted, always the same zone. "Jyzer's
trance." (An old attempt to name it, "Jyzer" being a
stenographic speed-brief of sorts for "journalizer" or
"J-izer": from the days when "Zone" was still "Exploring
Mentoka.")
    Maps on the walls, all featuring the M. zone. One
just for railroads. The fictional Carver County. Copy
of an authentic regional map circa 1790 with the Carver
Grant territory appearing on it as if it really had
been granted (I mean this was the primary regional map
in use worldwide at that time). And of course Mentoka
Falls and Lahontan and Wachute city maps and Mezzu and
U.M. campus maps, all hand-drawn and wildly conflicting.
                              *
    -- Just did the ink fill-up from the almost empty
bottle. Unthinkingly I reverted to a trick stumbled
upon years ago. Goes like this: hold the neck of the
ink bottle at a slant between the ring and little
fingers of your left hand (if you're righty); then,
grasping the barrel of the pen with the thumb and index
finger of the same hand, twist the ink-loading piston
at the top of the barrel with the first two fingers and
thumb of your right hand. This way you can tip the
bottle to pool all the remaining ink in one corner and
it's still possible to draw some up even when you're
nearly out. Lefties, reverse everything.
    Might almost be fictive G practicing up for his
first TA gig, tech writing, that paragraph.
    All week names again. Not much else. Too much
work at the office with two of the dayscopers out at the

same time (one sick, one on vacation). What to do with
the Mentoka tribe? How to work in some of their myths
and legends and realities? Surely Schoolcraft studied
them and Longfellow was inspired by them and that's one
source of the Hiawatha poem and therefore the name of
the train that tore through town when I was a kid (but
not through Gatewood when fictive G was a kid). And so
forth.

Also worked on the Mezzu pregame ritual involving
mascot Ollie Otter visiting the actually existing Silver
Mound to fashion the talismanic Silver Lance on which a
replica of that week's football opponent's mascot would
be impaled, with fraternities relay-running it back to
campus, torchlight parade, bonfire, fiery exhortations
demanding blowout victory. -- May sound absurd but
whole national epics are built on myths no less dubious.
And of course such stuff is still to be found right
here, the postmod or post-postmod (or however many posts
it is now) USA, in fact just about everywhere you look.

Again, the dangers of trying to fit too much into
the story. Fictive G wouldn't be much interested in
this kind of hokey rah-rah stuff. So it'll have to
shoulder its way into the background on its own and he
won't even take notice of that part of what he's
writing.

(Plane droning overhead. Horse sounds, dog sounds.
Strange creaking of shed frame as if something fairly
large were walking on the roof. Odd smell too, as if
this space opened into a locker room -- possibly a dead
animal rotting away down there beneath the floorboards.)

(Surprisingly, no one's ever broken into this shed.
Surely it would make a tempting target for any curious
kid in the area. Right now, though, it seems we're
between generations delinquency-wise. The rubble up at
the old "hippie hut" suggests that in more recent eras
the place has served as a hangout for hardcore dopers,
motorcycle bad guys, evil fornicators, maybe even
treacherous militia plotters. But just this week we
noticed a trio of skinheads moving into an outbuilding
on the horse "ranchette" that borders us to the

southeast. Glabrous domes and black leather with
lots of zippers, piercings, bad tattoos, evil leers.
So something may yet develop.)
      -- Scratching in this odd posture I'm reactivating
some long-dormant neck cricks. It's not good to be
tilting your head forward in the same position for so
long. And the "DREAM" cap, though buoying in other
ways, adds a few more ounces of ligament-straining
weight.
      Will I finally get going on the "Zone" rough draft
next month? Maybe not quite. Still a little too much
preliminary work to do. Next weekend is a long one
(Memorial Day) and I'm hoping to wrap up the naming
then. I mean I could keep going with this prepping for
years -- and have -- but I've got to break it off
somewhere. Set a firm date for the real opener.
      (More splendid timing: just now the bells of the
bible church start ringing and then neighbor Ben's table
saw explodes into action -- shatters them to bits, the
bell sounds, littering the yard with plaintively
tinkling spiritual shards, I'll say. And now the bells
and the table saw are both suddenly gone and we're back
to scattered birdcalls. -- A ringneck pheasant can
sometimes be spotted zipping along like a Road Runner
wannabe right outside my window here. And just last
week a strange pelicanlike apparition flapped down on
the road by the mailbox. -- And hummingbirds flit about
at all daylight hours. Blue jays flash. Woodpeckers
rat-a-tat. Owls whoo, though mostly at night. Geese
honk in the road. Ducks quack in raspy cacophony from
every puddle. Captain Brick three houses down herds
chickens when he's not off gambling or whipping the
local militia into shape (rumor has it). And he boasts
an authentic Filipina Dreamgirl wife, by the way, Jenny,
ordered from a catalog -- they go off to play bingo
every Thursday evening at the same time I leave for
work. His-and-her shotguns ride the rack behind the
front seat of their pickup. I doubt she's ever touched
hers, though, or at least not voluntarily.)
      "Sunday Morning Shed Dreams."

[The Origin of Jyze]

Beauty and sorrow here too. Wood. Lots of rough-
hewn wood. A slightly crooked stud rests at an angle
against the far wall and a spider web spans the acute
triangle where the two meet. Probably the spinner's
munching on an unfortunate (but winsome) little moth at
web central if I could see that far that finely.

-- I did read a Sunday magazine piece on the guy
who's keeping what's purported to be the world's longest
diary. As it happens he lives just an hour or two down
the road. And I'm not talking about brother Rob, though
he may be a contender himself someday on longest diary
and he's about that same distance away timewise
(depending on the ferry schedule). -- Except the last
I heard Rob was eking out no more than a few pages a
week. He said he was in a period of writer's block. An
unusual malady, I'd think, for a diarist. But that was
a while back and he's probably churning out the pages
again by now. At least I hope so.

-- The point of all this being what? Dust and
mildew, thin walls, in a few years if the termites don't
eat through them the beavers will. (Supposedly beavers
abound in the area though I've never seen one -- but we
often do hear trees falling in the woods for no apparent
reason -- which raises another of those thorny big-think
questions -- hereby quashed.) -- Or the thing might
collapse simply from the weight I'm piling into it. The
shed, I'm talking about. The shed dreams, no way.

(A big explosive sneeze right there.)

-- Now the trimmer mower starts up with its own
inimitable sputtering roar. That's Lady U. She's up.
She's in action.

I'm still wearing this goofy cap. Too bad the
mower seems to be heading off in the opposite direction.
-- Or why not chase her down so she can have her a wake-
up chuckle.

The jyzer breaks from his trance!

[Jyzeburst]

2.

     This time, thanks to the streetlight down by the
house, it's my own lengthening shadow that blazes the
uphill path to the shed. At two a.m. Through wet grass
freshly mown. As the Memorial Day weekend winds down,
its last few hours. To leave me exactly where I was
eight days ago, and in more ways than one.
     Well no. Progress has occurred. Not enough, but
some. And enough that I don't feel too bad about it.
One exciting afternoon in which new ideas kept popping
up eureka-style while I was supposed to be sleeping.
Madly jotting away on the pad at the head of the bed --
first time in a while for that. Transcribing those
ideas took nearly a full day -- transferring them to the
Mentoka notebook -- trying to fashion some links and
iron out some kinks.
     Could the word "jyze" be the key? It first popped
up two years ago but I let it slide. Now in rereading
the notes from that period it jumps out at me -- just as
it did in last week's entry. Even at the time I
thought: why the heck is this recidivating now?
     The slang dictionary and the big old unabridged
list only one "jy-" word, "jynx," and that's an obscure
genus of woodpecker (its adjectival form being the
savory "jyngine"). The practice of jyzism: you lay down
jyze in a jyzebook. Echoes from jazz, jive, gist, gyre,
jism, jizz, joss, jeez and lots more. Someone starts up
a jyzine. Someone's a jyzomaniac. Jyze, jyzed, jyzed,
jyzing. Best of all, the word works as several
different parts of speech: a jyzey jyzer jyzily jyzes
jyze. (Rhymes with the "lyze" in catalyze, I want to
note.)
     -- "In the Peking ferry I was feeling merry." The
radio's on, the so-called classic rock station doing to
me just what it's supposed to be doing nostalgia-wise.
"I sincerely thought I was so complete." Lord help me.

[The Origin of Jyze]

-- But it was more a matter of free-floating joy. This
sound could do it for me back then and it still can now.
What a simpleminded son of a gun I am. And more power
to me. Never lose your simple visions! (Where's that
"DREAM" cap? On the nail, you idiot! Look up!)
*

(Cap on.)
     Agony and anguish time this is? -- I think one
reason I'm frothing at the mouth to start the writing of
"Zone" is that then I'll have something real to write
about. As opposed to this dream world right here. It's
ideal, it's a dream, so of course it's sterile in
crucial respects. (You can't have it all, let's at
least admit that much -- or otherwise why write a word?)
     Soon, though, I'll have all kinds of life-
threatening craziness to zoom in on. I'll be able not
only to relive some terrific personal crises but to tack
on a few extra ones and to endow the whole with a
daunting panoply of meanings. Which isn't to say I'm
not nervous as hell about wrestling with all this. I go
back and forth on the thing, in and out, up and down.
But I wouldn't have it any other way. Not unless I knew
of a better way, one in which I could keep the
fascination and exhilaration while short-circuiting some
of the grief. But -- is the grief really grief? Nah.
I know it's not. I just want to have it both ways.
Wouldn't want anyone to think this was easy. (But it
is.) (No it isn't.)
     -- One thing that should soon be easier is the
scratching. Word from Mother is that a pen's on the way
up, and it's yet another X-BB just as promised. Ninety
bucks. Ol' Mom talked 'em down from one thirty. The
shop did have to order it from the factory, yes, but it
seems the factory is now somewhere in the U.S. Of
course the pen's not in hand yet. X brand has
snookered me more than once over the years. Still:
before much longer -- a week? a month? -- I should be
moving into a whole new realm of scratching in which
I'll no longer have to be fighting the damn scratcher so
much. "Scratching in the flow state." ("Call It

Jyze.") ("Call Me Jyzer.")
     -- The deep of the night is so narrow and shallow
this time of year. We're still in it but the first bird
might shatter it at any moment. Or it could be a
creature of the night will do it -- myself even.
     Jyze. Jazz. Got to jyze it up. Jyze on, jyzerman,
jyze me a J-book. "Now starring in 'The Jyze Zinger.'"
"Keep On Jyzin' Me...Till You Jyze Me Up."
     The new tentative schedule has "Zone" taking flight
about July 10, whenever the weekend is that falls in that
vicinity. Naturally I came up with a new hook to hang
the flight plans on. It'll be exactly two years, give or
take a day or two, after the start-up of the intensive
Mentoka research period. That came just after our return
from the trip to the coast for D's birthday, during which
the latest version of the old idea first grabbed me.
(Maybe I'd better officially note in here that D is short
for Dani, who is also Mel and Lady U).
     (The deep counter-counterminings of jyze -- flooding
the tunnels, so to speak, and blowing up the shafts. But
no. -- And who called jyze art anyway? Not me! There
is in fact only -- this. This scratchy splashy blotty
thing here is its own thing, whatever it's called. Where
it's going we'll just have to wait and see.)
     -- A slice of moon out there. Not yet gibbous but
of course glabrous as any skinhead. It's hanging above
the saggy old cedar barn and looks droopy itself as well
as blurrier than it should. Surely an omen of something
nasty weatherwise. We've had little to complain about so
far this year so we're due.
     To my right a stack of planks leaning against the
wall. They've been stationed there a couple of years or
is it three now? More bookcases they were intended for
but the plans had to be put on hold and that hold's
turned out to be quite lengthy if not permanent. Nor did
I get the cedar trim put up (around the windows and
door). Had to face the reality of how much time the
commute was taking. And besides: the shed was already
good enough without the trimmings, or, as I think now,
better. With them, too gingerbready.

[The Origin of Jyze]

(D's in full charge of housekeeping and yard work
around here. That's our deal. Otherwise this caretaker
regime would not have been possible and we'd still be
city folks, most likely -- and for that matter still are
anyway in all but physical location, and in a sense more
so than ever. Backwoods living can do that to you.)

     -- Meanwhile I keep on chugging back and forth to
the office and keep on scoping the pages, which as I
look at things means I'm not all that different from,
say, the author of a certain belatedly celebrated USAn
novel about a whale. That is, my life resembles his
during his sorry day-job period later in life at the
customshouse. Or -- whose?

                         *

     Where I was. Whiz break there. But yes, this
chair is bad for my neck. Not the chair by itself but
the combination of chair, jyzebook, and recalcitrant
jyzestick which demands the jyzing arm -- and how happy
I am with these proliferating jyze usages! -- demands
the jyzing arm be awkwardly angled to minimize skipping
and snagging, not to mention leak-opening jolts. (What
I meant was the chair is again where I am.)

     Next on the docket? Maybe break out the old photo
albums. I'm trying to probe the undying mysteries of
love. Or maybe not undying; maybe better to cite
necrophilia here. I've also got to get some more
plotting work done tonight and tomorrow morning.

     Perched atop my three pillows on the couch in the
libe, three lights on (overhead fluorescent -- not my
idea to hang that thing up there! -- desk lamp, table
lamp), the radio on low, the floor-to-ceiling curtains
closed (these in front of the big sliding pocket door,
so-called, apparently for no better reason than it's
installed in one piece, frame included, into a pocket in
the wall). Half a dozen large three-ring binders laid
out on the table and the couch, with lots more piled on
the floor. Big box of pens and markers, all kinds of
colors. Post-it pads of various sizes and hues. Three-
hole punch. Ruler that says "Glen's Ruler" right on it
and in official-looking white print. All these being

13

tools of the plotting trade.

That's how it'll be, is what I'm saying. Right now I'm still up here in the shed. -- Fictive G, though, where's he? That I've got to be figuring out pretty soon. Or else.

Rolling my head this way and that and listening to the ligaments pop. Thinking: fictive G is holed up in his garage garret apartment looking out on moon-silhouetted Parapet Bluff just across the darkly flowing Mentoka, he's sitting in a chair much like this one -- in fact, this very chair; why not -- and jyzing away at three in the morning. A class to teach tomorrow. A paper to write. A letter from Lady K to answer. And Saturday a drive up to Turtle Rapids to show off some family heritage (but not the closeted skeletons he hasn't even learned about yet) to the woman destined one day to become Lady S (as testified to by those same photo albums). -- May the jyze gods help this boy! The troubles he's about to bring down on himself!

-- Just realized I've been hearing some twittering out there. Absolute black is what I still see, though, except for the moon now higher and even more surreal as it abjures all earthly attachments. Perched near the top of the uphill trees to the east the birds have a much better angle on dawn and so I guess they must be seeing it. But regardless I'm done for the night.

3.

Wild ride. All week. No longer is the book "The Mentoka Zone," it's now "Jyzer." And no longer is the potential sequel merely its untitled self; like a tree struck dead-center by lightning it's now split into two: "Mentoka Dreams" and "Mentoka Ghosts." And the three together are the new Mentoka trilogy.

All kinds of explosives going off to cause this and as a result of it. A weeklong jyzeburst! No doubt about it: everything this G right here writes from now on will be vastly different because of it. And that goes for fictive G too, and also any other fictive G's that may come along later.

Just one more week though. Lots of weeks like this over the years. "Illumination Rounds." "Foudroyance." And now: "Jyzance!"

Downstairs this time. I'm too lazy to make it up to the shed. Too mentally exhausted to be able to say much of anything. All weekend I've been grinding, pushing myself to the limit -- sometimes wondering if my brain might shatter.

Seclusion is it. The next six months at least. The fiercest focus possible. (But this, what I'm doing right here, will be back. I've decided that too. In fact it will never be gone, because it will be doing its own jyzey thing in "Jyzer" as well. But after the rough of that is complete the jyzing will be back to real time -- i.e., jyze in its natural state.)

The nature of the breakthrough is almost self-evident from the new titles. Jyzing is what all these Mentoka books are about. For that matter, in its broadest sense it's what my entire adult life's been about: the conflict between that and fictifying on the one hand, between that and living a conventional loving and goofing and politicking and dollar-grubbing life on the other.

So what's next? Three more weeks of across-the-board prepping, that's what. "Final countdown." I have every reason to believe that by -- never mind. Boosterism threatens. Stomp it out.

-- Suddenly I realize the "Jr." at the end of my name (and fictive G's too) could itself be said to stand for Jyzer, and that this odd coincidence could be said to say it all. And for me, like it or not, it probably does say it all. -- And I want to say it does for fictive G as well, but in his case the confirmation is yet to come. He's still gotta show his jyze chops.

A second big breakthrough occurred when I stumbled on yet another better way to present Mentoka history. I was close to it before but not there and the frustration was driving me mad. Now I'm there. A plethora of frustrations and blockages may await me in the days ahead but none will be that particular one. And none will be so maddening, I'm sure of it. All the major structural problems for "Jyzer" and the new Mentoka books have now dissolved. -- Just how this could be, it's way beyond explaining. But then, no problem: jyze doesn't need to explain. Thank you, jyze gods, for your ruling on that!

True, I'm reminding myself of this lack of a need to explain (even explaining it to myself) way more than should be the case. But then it's still early in the Jyze Age.

(Recalling how comical it is -- though gut-wrenching too -- to flip through old notebooks in which I think I've solved this or that enormous problem regarding a writing project which a week or a month or six months later I've been forced to lay aside for the duration, in some cases right up to the present. What a massive junkyard I've strewn with these things.)

A giddy epiphanic moment also when I discovered Sandefjord Bay on Peter Island in the Sea of Amundsen off the coast of Antarctica. Or actually it's Peter I Island, discovered back in the 1820's by a Russian. But I'm gearing up to put a little fictional spin on this history to keep it afloat in the archipelago of "Jyzer" family facts and legends.

Here in the basement. Jazz post-midnight. Lilting out right now, lord help us, a sappy little tune I taught myself to play on the piano way back before Mentoka was even a twinkle in its parent's eyes (as far as I know, and I should since I'm him, the parent, agamic type, if that's the term, and I believe it is). -- Nor was jyze a twinkle then either, of course.

This chaotic scratching. Will I do any better with one of the new J-sticks? Will what comes out at that point, and from that nib, still feel like something called jyze? A good chance at least one of those X-BBs will arrive this coming week.

[The Origin of Jyze]

More serendipity: a few days ago I chanced upon a
stationery shop selling my longtime favorite brand of
ink. A brave little three-tier pyramid of boxed bottles
on a low back shelf and not even all that dusty. The
product name is slightly different now, true, but need
that matter? After all: it still boasts the same
magical self-cleaning formula. Sez so right on the
box. Also it never came in boxes before, which fact
doesn't worry me either. Probably this new version has
been on the market for years and I simply couldn't see
it because of the colorful new packaging. In any case:
I bought five bottles. One more and I'd've bought them
out.
     I'm still endorphing over all this. The swarm is
loosed. The night is forever kick-ass.
     And right here the plastic red ruler that until day
before yesterday bore the commercially printed words
"Glen's Ruler." After a little down-home tinkering with
an oil-based marker it now reads "Jyze Rules."
     Meanwhile friends and relatives are closing in.
It's that time of year again. Phone ringing all day.
Paul and Lori. Auntie Alice. Cousin Kar and the kids.
Warren and Mei. Two separate contingents of "Japan
Japanee." Also D's parents have announced a week's
expansion of their visit and so it'll now swallow up
most of August. Since the "library" here converts into
a guest room which they'll be staying in, and my study
is directly overhead and the ceiling is not soundproofed
and they've been unhappy with my late-night pacings in
the past, I'll be moving most of my operations back up
to the shed. Also may start going in to work on Sunday
nights again. We'll see. Fortunately (though it's no
accident) my night job gives me a good excuse to opt out
of over-the-top social stuff. Quite often D says she'd
like to devise a similar scam for herself.
     Not that I ever intended to become such a recluse.
Rather it's gradually turned into a necessity. True, I
could've chosen to go some other route. Because I found
D I could go this route. No doubt about it (I say over
and over): finding her was my luckiest break of all.

-- I'm fortunate also that a month or so back my two best pals from the graveyard-shift ferry runs went over to swing. I might've had to change ferries just to avoid them so I could focus exclusively on in-transit "Jyzer" prepping. Tom T. and Haskell. Love 'em both. However, for a while love 'em both from a distance. (There's still Lan but she's rarely chatty and usually sleeps on the bench opposite for the whole morning run and almost always catches an earlier boat in the evening.)

(Here's the greatest jazz singer of them all -- the accolade is close to unanimous -- in her perky early form, back when her accent and even her speaking-voice timbre were astoundingly like my own grandmother's, who couldn't sing at all but told a whole lotta fine stories on the radio in Lahontan: our only known family media personality and a late-blooming one at that -- and as Nana H. she'll soon be performing some of the same storytelling role over the airwaves in "Jyzer" as well.)

Lean back and stretch. Usual black sweatpants and heavy gray long-sleeve henley I wear on weekends. Even at the height of tourist season haute couture is not big in these parts.

-- The "Jyzer" comp books will have forest-green covers. I've already numbered the pages of the first one: 224 of them. I'm going with forest green because all the others are still cellophane-wrapped in packages of five. Well no, I shouldn't say that, I have a loose fuchsia (which I like least of all the colors) and even a black. For some reason I want "Jyzer" to have its own separate and inviolate color and it must be green.

Fictojyze series, that's to be distinguished from jyze itself. Same zone but different entrances. (And then within the fictojyze a kind of inner zone that will be a jyze zone for fictive G -- a/k/a Jyzer G -- but not yet a fictojyze zone. That might be a discovery for him in one of the later Mentoka volumes.)

-- Should I call the trilogy, all three volumes together, "The Jyze Age"? I'm thinking maybe yeah.

-- This week or next I might take off a day or two

from work if it appears the prepping is falling behind.
I might do it anyway. Isn't it the case that I'll now
be able to start up right on schedule no matter what
happens? I think probably so, but I guess I can't quite
believe it.

Squint. What time does that say? -- Wait a
minute, there's no clock down here. I'm suddenly
getting radios confused. Or confounded. Or whatever's
right. (Drat this indirection!)

-- The half-life of the J-book. I notice the
jyzing is now exactly halfway to half-life, to page 24
of 96 (just three 32-page signatures in this skinny old-
school comp book, as opposed to seven in the big fat
shiny new ones). So does this mean I'm about to stop
for the nonce? Hell no! I'm on a roll! And besides,
I'm not all that tired. It's two-twenty a.m., the DJ
chirps up at just the right moment, letting me know I
actually should be tired, or more tired.

The waves usually hit on schedule. But if they
don't they can sometimes be induced simply by thinking
about their delinquency. That's doubly true if
something important needs to be done.

Nothing like that in sight at the moment.

So should I overrule myself and put a cork in it
for now? (Let's see what the "Jyze Rules" ruler
decrees. -- The ruler says yes! -- Flipped it like a
Chinese fortune stick. Which is why the coffee table
boasts a new scratch. I think. Hard to be sure when
scratches are everywhere.)

Maybe I'll wander up to the shed. And yet --
there's so much to do up there I shrink from starting
anything. -- Which can no longer be a valid excuse at
this stage of the countdown.

*

(Thought as I was about to thirty this thing: the
Jr. at the end of my name could also stand for Joker or
Jester. Juggler. Juker. But Jyzer is still mainly it,
yes. Now and forevermore. Just how it is. -- "Thirty
it" came bubbling up from the long ago, newsroom lingo,
also inspiration for "Two-Star Chronicles." -- Endit!)

CHAPTER TWO

[What is Jyze For?]

1.

Another postponement. Admittedly I'm ashamed. Yet
I'm not. It's not even that I refuse to be. What I'm
doing I have to do. I'm under the spell.
So again I've slogged up to the shed. Pulled on my
knee-high rubber "barn boots" this time but happened to
come out between downpours. The heavy kind but they
don't last long -- the downpours, I mean, but it's true
for the boots too. Cheapos.
Crack open what was once the postjournal or PJ comp
book and it's now become a whole new book. JB comp
book, could say, a book within a book, just as this shed
is a shed within a shed. But the idea is simple:
reflect the new reality. From here on in it's all jyze.
"Scratching for the jyzone." Almost the same
slogan. The details on how it's different I expect to
start figuring out any minute now.
And it's back to jazz at the start. That classic
rock station is just too much, especially since I listen
to one much like it at the office (not because I
particularly like it but because I like it better than
anything else accessible there, and that ain't much --
downtown reception being notoriously poor).
-- So the postponement. What it amounts to is it's
taking some time to consolidate the gains of last week's
wild ride. Lots of things have to be rejigged.
Nonetheless it seems to be working. Better and better I
know who this fictive G is and how he jyzes and just

what's happening to him. Sez I. But who's to deny?
Main thing, I like jyzing his way.

For example, now he can be a blues lover again.
Little Bill's can become Nick's Blues Bar. "The best
little blues bar in all Mezdom."

I'll still be taking the plunge at the end of the
month. The orientation section is much simplified and
ready for launch. The idea right now is to have all
things in place for the first academic quarter (first
third of the book) before starting up what was once SIFT
and is now JIFT: "jyze in fictive time" -- this right
here being JIRT: "jyze in real time." Then a six-week
cruise before pausing again to set up the second
quarter, and so on to the end. That should come in or
around the second week of December.

Middle of another night in the woods. So be it.
This will be more truly jyzelike.

All week long when lacking anything else to do I've
been trying to pin down what this jyze is all about.
Eventually I'd like to work up a jyze manifesto. Like
that pamphlet on the shelf directly behind me, what's it
called? (He mulls.) "B-ism: A Manifesto," with "B"
representing a word I've forgotten except for the first
letter. Not that I remember much about the rest of the
manifesto either, other than the name of the very fine
poet who wrote it. Maybe nothing. "I do this I do
that" -- the only remaining trace. Nor do I intend to
swivel around and refresh my memory, at least not right
now. Can't even be sure I wound up liking the thing.
But do like the idea of a jyze manifesto.

-- More on that later or another time. Still a
long way to go before I can nail down this jyze thing.

-- Am I saying there's nothing else to write
about? Not at all. But then, isn't that the way things
ought to be? From nothingness, jyze!

Still no new pen. Upcoming is a paycheck week and
therefore I can drop by the pen shop again, because I'll
have the funds if one of the X-BBs has come in. The
shop might've been trying to call but because of all the
relatives and other acquaintances of varying degrees of

remoteness descending on the area, we've been lying low, often not answering. It's high tourist season!

     -- Karen A.'s picture may go up on the wall in here. I associate her death with Mamie Cummins's. I am Nick, my wild-ass bad-guy great-great uncle. This is a good way to get deeper into feeling the story and also to honor Karen's memory as well as Mamie's (Sadie's in "Jyzer"). I've been owing them both something like this for a long time. And the same's true for Lady K.

     With Lady S the matter's more complicated but probably not fundamentally different.

     "Mentoka -- the 26th State?" might be a work of history referred to within the book. The exact number it would've been I don't know. Better check it out. An item for the First Thursday meetings of the Mentoka Valley Historical Society, attended sporadically by fictive G as he pursues his roots for story-spinning purposes. (It does help, I think, to accustom myself to writing about all this as if it were real.)

     Another idea that just hit: have G find a chipped Wachute Sesquicentennial cup just like the one I picked up in the zone last year that's standing in front of me on the desktop now -- stumble upon it in a thrift/junk shop. For him what's special about it is that the celebration took place the year of his conception.

     Good stuff. The pile keeps mounting. Enough here for a dozen books. The key is to find a tone of voice and perspective on daily life for G that will allow some chunks of this good stuff to get into his story without undue strain. And that's what I've been working on all week. He's become a bit more unlike this G right here, me, at his age -- a little less social, a little more ingrown. A strong streak of that was always in me but I fought hard against it. Fictive G won't as much. Being a young dude of his time he'll be more skeptical, more worldly wise. This is an era of horrendous pandemics and impending ecocatastrophe, among other abominations.

     (Raining hard again. A dozen moths seeking shelter beneath the eaves on the leeward side, several with wings frantically -- audibly even -- whacking the

plexiglass demanding entrance or maybe just attention.)
    -- I did take two nights off from the office this week. Came up with the excuse that I'd stepped in a gopher hole and badly sprained an ankle. Not hard to fake because after tearing up my Achilles last summer I was limping pathetically for weeks and still am favoring it at times and yet have never used it as an excuse to take off from work. For almost eight years straight I didn't miss a single night. But that was mostly back when I was relatively well paid for this kind of job. And appreciated. Neither's the case now. Thus my intention is to use up my full complement of twelve sick days this year. All the dayscopers have done that since the beginning. I've taken the reverse tack of trying to make myself indispensable. Now I say: why bother?
    Am resisting the urge to apply a dab of Mating Call Deer Scent to my wrist. Little plastic vial here labeled with just those words in flowery blue handwriting. That vial too will be playing a key part in the Mentoka series. Both deer and mating are important in Mentoka, probably in that order; but for fictive G, and real G as well, gotta say, mating rules. -- Now I notice that about a third of the actual potion has evaporated since I bought it in the M. zone last fall. Could this have something to do with our local deer's love for rubbing against this shed? Probably not; they did it just as much back before the vial was here. -- But how do I know "just as much"? It's not as if I counted the little tufts of hair caught in the cedar siding before and after.
    (Some of this Mentoka stuff I might want to rethink. Nothing is set in stone. And even if it were, stones shatter, stones melt, stones turn out to be papier-mache illusions.)
    -- And here's my set of "Storybook" U.S. postal stamps, including one for "Little House on the Prairie." Of course I had to buy a full set to mount on the wall in here. In real life the "Little House" is just forty miles southwest of the ancestral digs. I drove over to check it out last fall. It wasn't much bigger than this

shed -- even looked something like it. I've never read any of the books in the series nor have I seen the TV show based on it, but it plays a big part in Mentoka-zone mythology. (The other three stamps feature stories I did read as a kid: "Huck," "Rebecca," "Little Women.")

Meanwhile I'm noticing I've been up here almost an hour and a quarter -- two minutes short of that (the clock always resets to 12:00 when I flip on the juice and it now reads 1:13) -- and though I haven't been pushing it at all I've still churned out a little over six full comp-book pages. Knowing this matters because most of the "Jyzer" entries will be limited to ten such pages and now I see fictive G would need only about two hours to write that many. He'll be very short on time, so this is good news. I was thinking he'd need three hours. -- But the average entry will be more like five comp-book pages, an hour's worth.

Says a button to the right of Popeye's old book of "Stories from Scottish History" (its red cover shrink-wrapped to keep out moisture) -- says: "Do you ever wonder if you've crossed the line between doing art & being Art?" Standard self-congratulatory arts stuff but the strange thing is I'd never noticed before what this button said. It's from that same set -- the "DREAM"-cap order -- and I've been staring at it uncomprehendingly for weeks now. -- And on another of the buttons the guy pictured wearing a T-shirt that says "I'm Art," he resembles way too closely Mr. Happy Face. Nor do I like his bermuda shorts or his skinheadishly glabrous dome. -- The same figure shows up on all three buttons, which I did vaguely know. -- But you've got to accept this. Whoever drew them up, at least that person wasn't out pushing electrotherapy for nonconformists. And that's only the first of a number of good things that could be said about these buttons.

(Trees roaring right now at +1:23. And just as suddenly not roaring and then roaring again, I can't keep up. -- But when the wind blows like this I still congratulate myself that the shed windows don't blow out (or in). I did one helluva job on those windows.)

[What is Jyze For?]

     -- Writing about having nothing much to write about
turns out to be a whole genre in itself. And I'm not
talking about Buddhist writing, though that may be
similar. In any case this genre right here, whatever it
is, is engrossing for this G who's pushing the J-stick.
Writing becomes really worthwhile only when you're
reduced to writing about whatever you have to write
about when you no longer have anything worthwhile to
write about. This is not strictly true. Obviously not.
But it's not without a loose, raw truthlikeness. It can
take you into some little-explored territory. Or maybe
it's better to say the territory is much-explored (dare
to say for one by a certain canonical nineteenth-century
French fictifier with his yen to write a whole book
about nothing) -- is much-explored, yes, but still can
be productive of freshness or newness because of the
person you must become to be able to explore it.
     -- Think this idea needs a little more work.
     But I've done enough for tonight. At +1:31. And
not even breathing hard. Ready to go another five or
ten pages should it be called for. But it's not. On
the contrary. Save the energy for "Jyzer" prepping;
right now that's much more pressing. (To write
"pressing" I guess unconsciously made me press old No.
3 a bit harder than usual because it just issued yet
another impressive blot.)

                              *

     (But do want to mention my feet have all along been
getting hotter and hotter in these boots. How could I
have overlooked that? It's to think about. Some secret
lurks there. And other places. Many. This is the
unexpected beauty of vagueness. Wiggly squiggly
overheated little secrets everywhere. Surely I'm on to
something here.)
     (Okay, and the B-word noted earlier starts with a
P, not a B, and it's "person." "If it does this like a
person, if it does that like a person, it manifestly
must be a" -- yes. The boy has B's on the brain.
"There is nothing like a double-broad. Nothing / in the
/ world....")

2.

Do I want to be doing this now? I don't. Do.
Don't. But what the hell, I'm doing it.
In a savage mood. Bite off the hand that jyzes
this right now.
Or: we'll see what happens. Basement of the
only real bookstore (ORB), foot of the stairs, west
side, away from the service counter. Footfalls up and
down, creaks from the ceiling. Applause from the
adjoining room. An author speaks.
So what's my gripe this time?
The center's not holding. The sides aren't
holding. Not even the holds are holding. But this is
all dull normal.
For one thing none of the new X-BB pens are here.
Now the pen shop's back to the old excuses: double-
broads aren't stocked in the U.S., the factory (which
Lowell and Cliff both insist is still in Germany) must
be consulted, containerloads are sent over only four
times a year. (Actually this last bit is new --
containerloads of fountain pens?) So who knows how long
it'll be. They say a week or two, making no sense at
all (a winged' container perhaps?). More likely it'll
be six weeks, two months. Or in the end I might get the
same old close-out story: the factory stopped making
them. But then why are they included on the most recent
price list? Saw it with my own eyes, the "BB."
To hell with it. -- Sure. Who am I kidding? I'm
counting on these goddamn pens. They'd better show up.
(It's embarrassing to be writing here like this. I
place my left hand blinderlike against my left temple
with fingers bent above both eyes to block out all
reactions of passersby. Also block out the glary
overhead half-globe lights focused on each table, this
one included. Each table a circus ring. Or each table
a table for a table dance. The jyzer is dancing. Ha!

-- Right now not too many others down here are dancing
either. Nor will the jyzer be not-dancing here for
long. It's a Friday night. He needs to show up at the
office sometime in the next couple of hours to get
started on the not-dancing there.)
     -- Last night I didn't answer the phone at work
because I didn't want to talk with cousin Kar. He's
still trying to ring me up even though I sent him a card
saying I'm in deep reclusive mode now, sorry, get back
to you when I emerge, if ever (but more diplomatically
phrased). Of course it could be he hasn't received it
yet. And now maybe I've gotten myself in trouble with
the office by not answering the phone. Maybe it was one
of the partners calling. Or dayscoper Doris, who's been
known to go whining to partner Fran about other scopers'
alleged deficiencies such as not answering query calls
from reporters. Probably I can wriggle out of it anyway
because I've generally been reliable as hell for years.
Nonetheless I'm burned up about this. Too.
     -- End of work-related digression that turned out
not to be so digressive, except to mention that this
tabletop, which is all I can see at the moment because
of the way I'm shading my eyes, is bright blue. And the
J-book, angled upward at roughly thirty degrees from
horizontal, is a much lighter, dirtier, grayish blue.
     Sometimes inspiration will stiff you. Any future
jyze manifesto must recognize this truth. (Here I
notice my coffee cup's been empty for quite some time.
Glass cup. Different brand of coffee from that of
earlier years in this joint but same cups. Same white
tiles on the floor, little ones an inch square. Same
ancient brick walls and columns, same not-for-sale used
books wedged into rows of floor-to-ceiling bookcases,
same rough-hewn bookcase wood, same exposed pipes and
vents overhead, same half-globe lights dangling -- and
refills still free too. I'm going for one right now.)
                           *
     -- Worst of all (I'm back), the "Jyzer" start-up
date keeps sliding into the future. Again and again I
find things that absolutely must be dealt with first.

One step forward, two back. Wild mood swings (not that
moods have never swung wildly before). Bummedness.
It's so stupid! But so's just plunging recklessly ahead
when you're not ready. And it's all up to you, nobody
else is telling you what to do. Not that there are no
pressures out there. However, I did vow to minimize
this kind of complaint in here. -- And pep talks to
myself, those too I vowed to tamp down. I'd find other
ways to pick myself up and light that goddamn fire.
    (Mother sent some old snapshots: Dad and me and
her, Kar Sr. and Julie, Hank and Windy, Grams and Aunt
Ida, the men all in uniform because they're home on
leave. It being January, Barb has recently been
conceived though probably no one knows this yet,
including the conceivers. Ida looks astoundingly
mannish, but I'm fairly sure Arlene was the so-called
butch in their longtime same-sex couplehood (which
presumably none of the others talked about, ever). I'm
a round-faced blond infant in Dad's arms, clearly not
too happy to be there. D says I don't look like myself
in this photo. "Who is this kid? Is that you? Where's
your chin? Didn't you have a chin back then?")
    -- Old No. 3 seems about to run dry. Hold it up to
the light so I can peer through the transparent band
located just above the nib -- or well above rather, a
good inch and a quarter -- let's be precise, damn it! --
no, still plenty of ink. But I'd better quit anyway and
hoof it on up to the office.
                *   *
    Trouble is this jyze form taking shape right here
is so seductive for the jyzer. For this very jyzer
who's also taking shape right here, yes, and made from
pretty much the same stuff. Thinking fictive G should
sometimes sound like this. More impulsiveness and
vagueness and meditative ire. Having the poor fellow
churn out acres of cheerful prose won't do at all.
    Just fourteen hours later and I'm seeing some
things a bit differently. Don't want fictive G, or for
that matter any G, to be dazzling. Don't want any of
those same G's to put the dynamite in. Fumbling and

stumbling is far better. A pathos in it and definitely
not too much triumph.

     -- This at my study desk. Just barely enough room
to lay out this J-book. Clock ticking tinnily.

     And what about "the zone"? Well, what zone? Do I
even know what it is? In "Jyzer" it's the turf but it's
also the trance, the flow state, the sense of being in
the groove. "Jyzer's trance" -- there it is again.
"Jyzone." Yes, I know such a thing exists, but I guess
it's a bit more contemplative than I'd been assuming. A
free-associational quality to it but also some thought
going on. Pauses. It's not exactly an unceasing flow.
It's not without its own hesitations, its own pain and
suffering -- yet somehow they're almost unnoticeable.

     Am zoning a bit right now. And have said just what
while doing so? That I don't really know what I've said
helps me believe in myself as a jyzer. Unless I stop
and think; then I know. But though I do stop and think,
it's a sideways kind of thinking that keeps me from
breaking out of the zone, and the knowing is sideways
also. -- But best not get all tangled up here.

     Fret and restless be, just because of how you sit
or lean! (A rambunctious trombone blaring on the
radio.) -- Trad jazz insists you must at all times
maintain contact with the melody, but jyze can also go
avant-garde or beyond. And will at times, I expect, if
only out of desperation. Which come to think of it is a
pretty damn good reason. And beyond avant-garde,
vagueness. And beyond that, nothingness. And beyond
that, I suppose, indifference, but we're not going
there. Jyze isn't. Maybe another time. Another era.

     Well. -- Geez, and look at all these books lined
up. To the left, to the right, behind and in front.
Stacks of newspapers. Crutches galore, all intended as
aids in fooling myself into believing I'm not merely
playing make-believe. That's honestly what it amounts
to. The not-pretending pretense. Not a whole lot
different from talismans and voodoo. A roomful of
dreamtime mojos. (Though there are other dimensions to
all this, namely those involving efforts to explore and

learn. I can't deny some things here are less than
wholly superstitious.)
     -- No no no. No self-laceration. Why bother?
Who's got the time?
     What can I do but keep honestly, earnestly,
"doggedly" (sister Barb's preferred term for how I go
about my fictive efforts) marching ahead? I mean that
literally: what else can I do? Nothing. It's turning
out this is the only pursuit for which I'm psychically
equipped. Simple as that.
     Well anyway, to hell with all the thumb-sucking,
simple or not; it's back to "Jyzer" prepping. And I
mean right now.

                    3.

     Bonus coverage! This is the new pen. No. 4, I'm
calling it. Its maiden voyage. Aptly enough (I guess)
aboard a ferry. Hot day -- first scorcher this year.

          ///// ///// ///// /////

     It seems to be working okay. Next to funky No. 3
it's maybe a little tighter and primmer and more proper
even though it's another double-B. Also, as I'm just
now realizing, best not to tilt the thing quite so far
rightward as I have to do with No. 3. But not a skip so
far and no leaks either -- as we hit open water.

          ///////////////

     For weeks I've been haunting the P.O. box. Finally
today the package arrived while I was asleep, but
arrived at home, miraculously almost, because Mother had
given her pen shop the wrong address, combining our P.O.
box number, which by a quirk of postal gerrymandering is
in one zip code, with our street address which is in

another, even though the two are just blocks apart in
the same tiny town. Or never mind the "almost" --
miraculously is how it arrived, period.

     And then D had some fun with me. Tearing open the
box I found a gift-wrapped package inside, aptly pen-
shaped, a big blue bow adorning it. Ripped it open and
inside was a schlocky old cartridge pen with an extra
cartridge which was ninety-nine percent empty. Tacky
little traces of blue clinging to the inside and that
was it for ink. -- Chased her around the house as she
howled gleefully. And me still mostly nekkid, wearing
just the orange henley I slept in.

     And then she brought out the real box, the one with
the X-brand logo, which is not literally an X, of
course, but welcome anyway. And how!

     So here it is. (Am I here? Where I am! Because!
-- Or why bother with causation anyway? -- Nor need it
all be somber or bereft of nonsense. This is jyze!)

                    G G G G

     Could this mean "Jyzer" is back on the serendipity
track? I'm believing it. Did even before -- to wit,
moments after finishing up the scowly prior entry I came
across a review of the key document of them all: the
travel journal of the first Eurusan explorer of what
would one day become Mentoka. Some two and a quarter
centuries after its first publication it's being
reissued just in time either to upstage or to set the
stage for my warping of it in "Jyzer."

     And over the weekend a lot of the blockages gave
way. Why now and not some other time I don't know, nor
do I regret having learned what I learned while blocked.
I'd like to think I've now crossed the threshold. If
only just barely, I know enough to begin.

     (Huge white dry-docked cruise ship hovering aloft
like a retro spacecraft to the right, we're coming in.
Orange maritime cranes in squawking, wing-flapping,
pterodactylian disarray. A big chug and here's yet
another massive blue freighter stacked high with

orange, most of 'em, containers like an ambulant island,
we're angling behind it and buffeting noticeably now in
the wake of its laboring stern tug. And the baddest
mountain of them all is hulking off to starboard
wearing double lentricular cloud leis, as if it had
blown two concentric volcanic smoke rings and they'd
settled down around its super-thick wrestler's neck.
Wow, some sweet day it is!)

                    *   *

    Now back at the blue table -- not the same one at
the foot of the stairs but farther to the rear, in fact
in the far corner by the big upthrusting of ancient
pipes where I often holed up during our years of city
living (meaning those in this city) -- and I'm thinking
this week's blue-table mood will not be at all like last
week's.
    Just ordered the new edition of the aforementioned
travel journal. Happily it's being published in the
U.S. as well as England, meaning it'll get here much
sooner and also I might see a few more reviews. And
maybe they'll open up some new pathways.
    Should "Jyzer" be the screed of a leaky pen? It's
to be expected no doubt but I'm missing the
eccentricities of old No. 3. (Forking at a dish of
apple cobbler as I write -- making a mess of it because
the forking is left-handed.) For "Jyzer" it might even
be best to stick with No. 3 -- its insatiable demands
make for quirky diversions and hang-ups which could
then become part of what it's all about. And an excuse
for bad writing, grunginess, broken-off entries -- all
sorts of troublesome things that might be just what the
jyzer ordered in certain realms and passages.

                X X X X X X X

    (But I can't let Mother know. She's so pleased
with the notion of my doing the draft with the pen she's
bought for me. And I like the notion myself. So if I
stick with No. 3 for "Jyzer," maybe I'll say it too was
a present from ol' Mom, though one from long ago. And

have the young Jyzer G grump over how he's bashed it up
in the four years of collegiate high living since.)
        -- And thought some more about jyze. What's it
really all about? What's it for? Etymology of the
word. Possible connections. Urjyze and protojyze.
Great protojyzers of previous eras who didn't even know
they were protojyzing. Jyze strategies. Nature of jyze
fiction and jyze poetry. Relation of jyze fiction to
real-time jyze, JIFT to JIRT. Ecojyze and ethnojyze.
-- But regardless of its fate in the world I'll keep on
doing it. "Born to Jyze." Flat fact. "Jyzo ergo sum."
"Cacoethia jyzendi." "Solvitur jyzulando."
        On a roll here. Guzzling root beer from a fine old
brown bottle. Lucky bottle maybe. I might even take it
home with me rather than toss it in the recycle bin.
Make it a memorial to the dawning of THE JYZE AGE.
        The new J-stick. Flipping back to the opening
entries I see it's indisputable, old No. 3 has a vastly
heavier and more picturesque flow.

/ / / / / / / / / / /

Both nibs are double-broad but No. 3's is far broader,
most likely from being dropped on the floor a few times
although maybe just from being pressed relentlessly
against nib-unfriendly paper. "For years on end."
(Picturing years as upright slabs of marble and the J-
stick as a chisel.)
        Upstairs I was thumbing through a book on
"journaling" (dread word). In recommending blank books
the author reveals a dislike for those whose paper shows
too much "tooth." Means it bites into the nib and makes
the ink flow, I guess. She says avoid tooth because the
ink will tend to bleed right through the paper. But me,
I say hooray for tooth! Bleed-throughs and the ensuing
distractions and confusions, they're the JB's pajamas!
        So yes I think I'll try to stick with old No. 3.
But: not for this kind of use right here. Now I have a
J-stick that will travel. This quality makes its lack
of leakiness tolerable. As does the much more legible

writing it tends to produce (which I'd much prefer it
didn't, true, but legibility still has its advantages).

     Delight doesn't really fade. -- I even pressed a
red dot atop the cap so I can ID this new one at a
glance. Its "nombre de plume" is written in indelible
marker on the dot just in case I forget what the red
means. Soon, I hope, I'll be needing more dots of
different colors. Not for No. 3, though; that one, with
its cummerbund and gluey pits and outcroppings, would be
recognizable anywhere, maybe even from fifty feet.

     Might return later tonight just to show it's true I
can't resist. (Also must note right now: delight is
harder to "inflect through self." Yet why shouldn't it
count as attitude? Think of all the notables down
through the ages with whom it does! -- But think too of
the times ahead, the ones we're fated to live through or
more likely expire from. And then get a grip on
yourself and hunker right back down.)
                    *   *
     Yawning. High energy this will not. [Be.] Or
it's improbable but best to rule nothing out just yet.

     Hiked up here and then worked four hours scoping a
dep. Night of the solstice so it just might be the
shortest of the year (if last night wasn't) and I still
have to squeeze in a couple of hours of shut-eye. Right
here, on the conference-room carpet. (But this is not
the same conference room I was crashing in five years
ago. That one, if I stepped over to the window here I
could look straight into it, or almost, up one floor a
diagonal block to the southwest, an unobstructed view --
and I have no memory at all of ever looking from there
over this way, into this room, but I probably did. Was
some jyzer of an earlier iteration at work here then?
Did we wave with villainous complicity across the gap?)

     Big full moon just barely visible through the black
semi-opaque sun shade. Hiss of air conditioning. The
usual street screams and cries floating up seventeen
stories. Bus accelerations. Backfire or gunfire,
always hard to tell which is which. Tick of my windup
alarm clock (whose hour hand is about fifteen degrees

out of kilter, thus making for tricky alarm-setting).
     My sleeping bag rests atop the oval conference
table (yup, the same table as in all previous offices of
the nightscoper era). "Magic carpet." An electric
blanket too, but this time of year no need for the
electric part even with the air conditioning on high.
Lights out and I'll drop out of sight beyond the far
edge of the table. If someone pops in for a maintenance
or security inspection, as occasionally happens, they
won't be able to see me down there; they'll think I've
stepped out for a snack or a constitutional or maybe --
more likely -- to score some of the good stuff. Almost
every night I rack out like this, so over the years
there's been a whole lotta rackin' going on.
     Several times tonight the phone rang. I ignored
it. It was early enough I could comfortably let it be
thought I wasn't here yet. If this leads to trouble, so
be it. One or more of the calls might have been Mother
checking up on the pen. Her I'm not trying to avoid.
     Can of warm guava juice. On arrival I rushed to my
station to type up some new "Jyzer" notes and neglected
to put the juice in the fridge. Warm it tastes more
like it does right off the tree (and I know this because
a guava tree grows in the U family's side yard).
     Of course on the way up I'm always hoping the
workload awaiting me will be light. But if it is, I
worry I'll soon start looking expendable. My position
here is nowhere near as secure as it was, say, five
years ago. This is partly because of "technological
advances" and "industry trends" but mainly because I've
gotten more and more disgusted with the ass-kissing I've
had to do to stay in favor. At this point I mainly try
to keep contact with any of the day crew, partners and
reporters included, to a minimum. Encounters with the
night crew I don't usually mind too much, but then I am
the night crew. There is no one else. "Boot up the new
crew, same as the old crew."
     -- Twirling my thong sandal by the thong. Bump
bump bump. I did make off with that root-beer bottle.
The Eurusan explorer's journal should be here in two

weeks, the clerk said, so maybe in time for the "Jyzer"
start-up (fingers crossed -- and not ink-stained
anymore, by the way; they're curiously pristine, almost,
except for, I see now, some delicate black webbing on
the callus, the pen "sidesaddle," index side of middle
finger, right hand, directly behind the nail -- these
the remaining traces of No. 3's last whirl).
    Nap time, it's here.

CHAPTER THREE

[The First Law of Jyzodynamics]

1.

    New idea. Will it jyze? Maybe only like this.
How to blast through the last few barriers.
    I'm trying to be vague and strange anyway. So why
not write the thing straight? Or almost so. Close
enough so that it can always drop back into present time
(though in a vague way) if stuck. Later on I can strike
any of the present-time stuff that doesn't work. And if
that means striking it all, just regard the striking as
a means to an end -- a kind of discarded scaffolding.
    "Straight jyze, no chaser."
    Consider it done. For starters at least. Which
means pretty much I've already started. -- Hopefully
it won't be clear it's a grizzled vet J-sticking (much
like pogo-sticking) back across the years. Or not too
many years anyway. Could be this fictive G fellow is
himself "scratching it out in dysquility" a year after
the fact or something like that. Or just revising, say.
But doing it as fiction. JIFT.
    Could be the missing wire that allows the juice to

flow. Feels that way right now. Just patch it in!
     (where is this? Back to jazz, cushions, etc.)
     The challenge feels worthy again, yes, rather than
merely daunting. Force-feeding might lead to good
things. The oddly disjointed reflexiveness might serve
to deepen the story (give it that layered feeling). At
the very least it should heighten verisimilitude.
Evasive I'll be and dissimulative as well -- as hell --
no question, but no longer will I be engaging in flat-
out pretense. Scrap all fabulism! Instead: go for
artful. If it works. Or inartful if it doesn't. But a
good chance it will work -- one of those if not both --
and a good chance either or both will be a hoot to try.
     I'll do it. Do it all the way to the end (I do
believe) with the sure knowledge I can always go back
and change any goddamn thing I want to, including all
repetition (that again!). In those dubious change-
demanding areas simply make it all vague and open and
nonspecific and cryptic enough to pass.
     what I want more than anything is to have the rough
to work on. What I'm proposing now is the best way I
can think of to get there fast. And it might yield
unexpected gems and wild new rides.
     (I knew an idea was about to pop up. I can always
tell by the way I find myself puzzling and drooling
almost, unable to do anything else. Except flip
through, say, this JIRT right here, mulling and musing,
looking for I don't know what and hoping to find
something more or less accidentally right on the mark.)
     Don't want to neglect any of the other stuff. The
jyzone. The attitude. Push it hard if that's what it
takes. Be raw. Nurse that hurt. (Put a hurt on
yourself.) If you stick a finger in it you should get a
jolt. And be able to think of little else.
     Okay, that's the idealized version. But still. Or
better to say it this way: no. No but not no. Yes!
     So there.
     And nowhere else.
     (Those calls earlier in the week, they were Mother.
Some if not all. Wanting to let me know brother Jeff

had gotten married again. "An impulsive little jaunt
down to the justice of the peace." Today I ordered a
wedding present for him and Angie, a matched pair of
hummingbird whirligigs. Eight bucks. Perfect.
Identical except in color scheme to the one I bought
last week for Barb to go with the life-size duck.
I'll personalize all three with decorator pens and
off they'll whirl -- or just say hum.)

   -- Mother took another nasty spill. Her tailbone's
acting up. It sounds bad. But her health's sounded bad
so often for so long I no longer have any sense at all
of how alarmed to be.

   (This afternoon a bold new deer loping around the
yard nibbling at the dahlias and other choice items.
When we yelled it went highstepping off with pacerly
grace but soon reappeared. All along its jaw was
ruminantly a-grind as if to produce a huge pink bubble.)

   -- Oh but this could be very interesting now.
I'll be exploring even more than I'd realized. (And
stacks of new books piling up. One on the lethal
fantasies of the invader race, which is to say, of
course, us, i.e., USAn Cawks, Eurusans. And a second
one with a kinky angle on primal scenes.) Might even
recapitulate the whole J-stick business. Old No. 3 for
home use only because -- well, same reasoning. (Will
this take away from other magical symbols? The deer-
scent mating potion? It's something to guard against.)

   -- But manic days. So that means pumped moments
too. Jyze thoughts. Jyze plans. More enticing notions
cropping up for a jyze manifesto. Mulling the rap
dimension. Performance jyze. Improv jyze. Slam jyze.

   (One very bad day: a leaky soft-drink can in my
backpack, the main three-ring "Jyzer Notes" binder
soaked, every single page cola-washed at the bottom and
upward an inch or two, scores of notes blurred almost
beyond recognition -- but it's not really a disaster,
just a big annoyance, and no fun drying out all those
pages and relettering the band of faint note traces.)

   (I hear booms and creaks. Is this another
earthquake? We had one about three weeks ago, epicenter

some fifteen miles west of here. D said Fred the cat
jumped up and did a weird jig on his hind legs. If I
felt it at all down at the office it was a few extra
bumps during a magic-carpet ride, as if a convoy of
unusually heavy trucks or perhaps National Guard tanks
were passing down below. -- But no more signs right now
of a quake. Possibly a couple of the huskier local cats
were chasing each other up on the veranda roof. Or
raccoons. Or deer for that matter, who knows. We're so
far off the beaten track that the likelihood of it being
an urban kind of peril is next to nil (except maybe for
the new skinheads, true -- knock on a glabrous dome).)
   -- Thinking yes, many missteps ahead, many big cuts
and redos. But that's okay. We're talking jyze here!
   I hadn't expected a revelation as fine as this.
Pinch myself. But...will it all dissipate by tomorrow?
   Regardless all things look different now. Again.
Indeed as they should. Because that's the First Law of
Jyzodynamics.
   (Tonight I came across a review of some
pseudonymous gay guy's protojyze, a compression of
fifty-odd volumes into one, a "failed" writer who could
be said to resemble me, I guess -- damn it anyway -- if
none of the projects I've completed up to now ever
amount to anything out in the real world. The reviewer
derides the protojyzer's line about "nothing much has
happened in my life for the past eighteen years" (not an
exact quote). Hmm, I thought, I could almost write a
line like that about my own life. Perhaps even have.)
   -- Took up this J-book strictly on impulse tonight
and will put it down the same way. Yet to find myself
in a whole new place. Delighted to be here. Wondering
what the inevitable doubts will be when they hit as they
surely will (being inevitable). Thinking whatever they
are I'm not likely to want to retreat. Seem to have
broken through into a new dimension from which there's
no way back -- some of the old notions about differences
between fictifying and nonfictifying suddenly appearing
way too simplistic.
   So maybe someday I'll look back upon this as having

been one heck of a fine night. Is there any way I can
ever find this night regrettable? That I sat around
obsessing over such things at such and such a time in
such and such a place when I could've been doing this or
that here or there (maybe)? -- Can't see it, no.

*   *

(This is a tryout at the office. No, at the pen
shop. It's hard to get used to the idea of writing with
one of these brand Z's even if I've tried others before.
It works pretty well, though. Not that I recognize the
writing as my own. But -- try angling down a bit. Try
a twist to the left. No. Twist to the right. Stand
up, sit down. Go fast. Go slow. Bop till you....
Jyze till you're.... What's the use? Does utility
matter anyway? Who can tell? -- Try to compress.
-- Try again. -- So maybe I'll take this one too as a
backup. Can't be sure but presumably it would
eventually sing. Or if not, moan. Or cry uncle.

//// X JJJ G JYZER JIFT JYFT JYF

Maybe. Probably. Put down a deposit on it? If I do,
will they have everybody and her brother shaking the
thing down? $228 is the price and that includes the so-
called "twenty percent off." Well, let's see.)

*   *

Hey, check this out! The reworked pen is back!

///// G /////
NO. 2 NO. 2 NO. 2

All right! I'm pumped! No. 2 is pumped! (I think
I was calling it No. 2, wasn't I?) (Writ atop a
newspaper vending box a block from the pen shop.)

*   *

-- Sir Jyze-A-Lot really cranking it out today.
Flashed my new monthly pass, now I'm aboard the
passenger ferry. It's the fast one, yes it is. Rarely
do I see it anymore. Only a dozen passengers scattered
on two decks, surprising for a holiday weekend.

40

Lowell the scamp, he scammed me. A classic and oh did I bite. Not until I'd agreed to buy the brand Z and was about to walk out the door did he reveal that my repaired brand-X No. 2 had come back from the factory (earlier he had implied it wouldn't be in until August, just like the new one I ordered). No doubt he was afraid I'd never go for the $228 brand Z if I knew my old M-nib pen was back and the repair of the clickers and reconfiguration to a double-B would nick me, combined, only eighteen bucks (after tax!).

But he was wrong. I would've gone for both regardless. Just in case.

(Fast ferry not so fast today. Just sitting here. Maybe the missing passengers know something we don't.)

This newly repaired one I think I like better than No. 4. So far anyway. A little more flow and a lot less stiffness. Maybe the repair person at the factory genuinely cares about pens, whereas No. 4 just rolled down an assembly line, possibly fully automated. Or it could be mostly a matter of aging like good wine since I bought No. 2 roughly six years ago.

Might have to go with it for "Jyzer" and fib to Mom. This would be for strictly unsentimental reasons. No, fib for sentimental reasons, go with No. 2 for unsentimental reasons -- or so I say. They're actually mostly sentimental too, I suspect. -- And then carry No. 4 with me as a backup, so it's always right there (here) on the jyze scene. (And it'll get the best ID dot, the green one, and I'll put a new red one on No. 2. And I think I'll call it No. 5, since with a new BB nib it's really a whole new pen and the thing about its being No. 2 is a myth anyway, I'm almost sure.)

For old No. 3 it'll be retirement with full honors to a prominent place on the shed windowsill. Or maybe even on the study desk where it can oversee the drafting of "Jyzer." (And in a pinch, should all the newer X-BBs go haywire at once, it could fill in just fine.) ---

*

(Finally casting off twenty-five minutes late. A crew member didn't show up and a replacement had to be

called in from afar. This I just overheard.)
    The other pen, the brand Z -- the "deluxe
instrument" -- is strictly for deep reserve. A lotta
bucks for a little peace of mind, but I'll take it.
    -- We're zipping along on our twin pontoons. Weird
stormy weekend. Sun out at the moment but legions of
storm clouds rumbling about in plain sight, with at
least one hissing out forked lightning tongues which
you hardly ever see around here.

NO. 5 is /////////!!!

I'm pleased. I'm delighted. I've got a tag team of
X-BBs and a backup tagger's due in August just in case.
    This being D's birthday weekend I'm also loaded
down with gifts for her and various gag/party items.
Also I'll be picking up some goodies at the farmers'
market at the home port. And a few more of those four-
buck wooden hummingbird whirligigs, of which, like J-
sticks, it seems I just can't get enough. (Mom also
wanted to pay us a visit up here in August and I had to
veto that. I felt bad about it but I think she
understood. I can't let myself be jolted out of my
rhythm now when I've got it going so good. Just having
the U's staying with us for nearly the whole month will
be jolt enough all by itself.)

/////////////////////////////

    -- But will it jyze? Oh yes it will. Looks good.
Looks powerful. You go, NO. 5! Looks like a Mezzu
Silver Otter flexing in a black-and-silver away uniform.
And feels just right. Feels scratchy-smooth and shows
good flow. (Can anything else matter?)
    Well yes I'd say so. Because here I am. Am I
here? I'm here! It's uncanny!
    -- Rounding the last bend. Two TVs blaring. A
bathroom urge. No, head. It's right behind me. (Just
hope Mother doesn't go to her reward in the meantime
after I've turned down her plea.)

2.

     Shouldn't be doing this. It's bad. I know it.
Just can't help myself.
     Should be sleeping. If not now, soon. Instead the
itch is upon me. This is what I must be doing. "This
right here." This is how "Jyzer" narrator G is thinking
too. Sittin' in the railroad station. Just sittin'.
Don't need no ticket, ain't got no destination -- except
cranking out the jyze with the new No. 5.
     And me right here in the scope-office inner
sanctum, the small conference room at the center of all
the other rooms. Me in black gym shorts and sleeveless
green henley and that's it. We're into high summer now.
You work graveyard and you're the whole crew, you can
play beachcomber at the office.
     And again little work for me to do here. Four of
the past five worknights the same. Tonight punch in a
few corrections and do a stack of read-ons and a dozen
backups and run the streamers and that's it. Not a
single page of scoping. Might take all of ninety
minutes.
     Never mind the perils of this. Later for those --
when and if.
     -- Bizarre feeling as I jyze away. The conference
room is set up for a videotape deposition. Little wire
microphones perch like praying mantises on the table,
one for each chair. The video camera rides its tripod
on the far side and is pointed right at where I sit: the
witness chair. The little red light is on. Testify!
(And the air-conditioning is hissing and in the other,
larger conference room, a slice of which is visible from
here through the open door, the big red telescope is set
up in its usual spot but pointed out at the water and
not down at the infamous "meat rack" roof deck a block
over -- meaning clients, most likely, or potential
clients, and not dayscopers or reporters or partners,

used it last.)

To put in four hours' work I could arrive as late as two a.m. So that's when I'll officially beam myself down from the jyzosphere. Unless, of course, somebody important walks in. Could happen too, but at this hour it's not very likely (which of course has always been a major attraction of the job).

And how's the prepping for old "Jyzer" coming along? Just fine. It keeps darting off on useless tangents -- resisting, yeah -- but that's okay, because for the most part it seems to be heading in the right direction.

A bit of perspective opened up at one point. I thought enough about "Mentoka Dreams" and "Mentoka Ghosts" and how I might go about restructuring them as a result of the split-up of the former projected single sequel that suddenly "Jyzer" looked like a lighthearted and innocent introductory volume. Many of the up-close particular "Jyzer" problems I was wrestling with shrank immediately and some all but went away.

-- Rushed eight miles to the nearest drugstore this morning (and then eight miles back) so I could fill up the "party zone" in our so-called parlor with "balloon people," i.e., helium balloons painted with clown faces, each attached by ribbon to a floor-scraping weight.

Good, I can sense now this will not have to be a long entry. The end is already near. I'll be able to get some sleep after all.

-- Just be happy, jyze guy, you've got a well-stocked bench of eager backup J-sticks ready to bound into the ring should the one already there show signs of tiring. (But no, we're going to go with No. 5 for a while no matter what just to make sure it's properly broken in. I'm pressing it hard to speed up the process. Even caught a paper fiber in the gap between nib halves a couple of times. -- I still marvel at how funky old No. 3 used to feast on those fibers: scooped 'em up and gobbled 'em down.)

Video eye staring. Wotta trip if it were actually recording. Should I stand up and do a striptease? The

only video trace of me left for history (unless one of
those naughty X-rated tapes from Lady S/Lady V days
survives, which I suppose is still a remote possibility)
(though I don't have any left myself, drat it anyway) --
but here he is, contempo Jyzer G hard at it. Observe.
The first known videotape jyze session. -- And G-rated!
     End of exercise. (Penultimate? Ultimate pen?
Hold it up -- wave it aloft -- close this down.)

                         3.

     This is it. Last weekend of brainstorming "Jyzer."
In the past month or two the thing has grown enormously.
Also shifted. Deepened if I'm lucky. Tightened up
conception-wise for sure.
     But the growing's got to stop. It could easily go
on forever. Or until I tired of it -- had to abandon
it. Fiction hypertrophy. It's happened before.
     So this last night of letting off steam. (Back
where jyze first burst into being. Grooveyard. D all
tucked away. Contempo G perched atop the same old ever-
funkier cushions.)
     Came across "Ministry of Culture Approved" at the
rubber-stamp shop last night. Couldn't remember whether
I already had it. I'm still not sure. Last time I
stumbled upon it they were out except for the beat-up
display model and I ordered one. Can't recall if it
ever came in or, if it did, whether I picked it up.
Probably it did and I did. In that case I'll have two.
Can do tricks using different colors. Can elaborate
still further the fancy rubber-stamp tattoo on the front
inside J-book cover. All these being things fictive G
would also go for, I hereby decree.
     (Fury over another office power play by a dayscoper
operating in real time. Disgust. But never mind.
Actually what bugs me most is how hard it is to get
something so piddling out of my mind. The waste of time
and energy. It's not enough to remind myself what's

really important here. What's this job for anyway.
Keep focused damnit. But you can't always do it. You
obsess. It's your livelihood! -- Never mind.)

    Still hanging around, the balloon people. When you
walk by they don't just sway and nod, they scrape along
sycophantically in your wake, drawn by air currents.
Something fascinating about this. Ghosts in the house.
Clown ghosts. If you're going fast enough one or two of
them will chase you right up the parlor stairs and peek
in when you're hunched over on the throne. Or in D's
case, squatting on it old-country style. That happened
earlier today, eliciting from her a rare super-high-
decibel laugh-shriek -- reminding me of our earliest
days together -- followed by elaborate mutual
condolences and eventually a bout of compensatory
hossplay in bed (because we still got game here at U
Acres, yes we do) (and this a birthday encore).

    (Fred the cat just strolled in. Unusual for this
time of night.)

    A notorious dictator dies. An important figure in
my life, surprisingly enough. No one ever would've
predicted it. But then who would've imagined his
countrywoman Lady S coming onto the set, that is, mine?
(Same goes in a way for Ladies V and U, but less so,
and for the simple reason that they followed Lady S.)

    Will this style carry me in "Jyzer"? I don't see
why not. Needless to say (but obviously not entirely) a
great deal rests on how it lends itself to revision.
The running notes contain lots of worthy stuff that
clearly won't make it in on the first go-round. I even
like to suppose these notes have some intrinsic
interest. For sure I've put in more work on them than
on any prior research project.

    A new set of bold color markers for chart making.
I'll be drawing up some new ones, "post last rehearsal
type," this weekend. Also clearing space in my study.
The desk up there is stacked almost to the ceiling with
papers and books. And so's the rest of the room.
Mentoka-zone books. Railroad mags. Boxes of period
mags. Unbelievable accumulations. How research can go

on forever and never stop being engrossing and even
enrapturing. Nor ever stop generating the illusion that
the next item unearthed will be the most crucial of all.

(Tiny green bug dipsy-doodles by my nose and
suddenly swoops straight down to land at the base of my
left thumb. Almost as if it had a flight plan and a
schedule to meet. The bug being nearly transparent
physically but not so psychically, meaning as to motive.
-- Didn't stick around for long though.)

String of firecrackers going off in the night.
Real ones. Distant. Last twitches of the glorious
back-to-back holiday: Independence Day/Lady U's B-day.
Our skinhead neighbors have been back at it too, though
a shade more decorously than before. Perhaps they fear
excessive commotion will be misinterpreted as patriotism
(and around here, rightly so). Or maybe they've just
been mostly elsewhere.

Little green wooden hummingbirds with white chests,
red heads, yellow beaks, white wings. Forever standing
still like what they are even though the wings spin
freely with the flick of a finger. "Stand Still Like
the Whirligig." "The Jyzer at the Foot of the Ladder."
("Up with a Yank, Philosopher Manque.")

What's the far coast declaring passe' this week?
Oh how the otters laugh in the night, especially when
the moon is full (you can hear the splashes too). -- I
mean from right here you can. As the woods turn russet
and the ghosts slip silently from tree to tree like
balloon clowns but with polished silver lances a-glint.

-- Next time for JIRT, say about five months from
now, I'm guessing I'll be coming at it from a whole new
place. And feeling this impulsive exercise that started
out as the equivalent of a warmup scratch pad and then
morphed into jyze has served me well. Certainly do hope
so.

Any incantations, now's the time. The force be
with me, the edge upon me, the -- what? All those go-
get-'ems. Summon the lot. Strap it up. Fire out.
Elbow nastily. Squeeze that J-stick until it bleeds.

CHAPTER FOUR

[A Jyze Swerve]

1.

All right, kwikjyze. One last time I can't resist.
Because I've got something. It's hard. It's genuine.
It checks out. Which is to say: the thing is underway.
It's finally happening.
     Took lots of years if I'm to be strictly accurate.
Let's say about five since the last authentic start-up,
I mean all original stuff seen afresh and anew.
Something like that. Could be a couple more or maybe
one less, depending on the slants applied.
     -- Right on schedule it happened, though late by
earlier schedules. Who cares. Whatever it takes.
     (Creaking floor: that's the lady doing dance
stretches upstairs. Fresh breeze blowing in through the
wide-open pocket door at dusk. Me barefoot and wearing
just gray shorts and a white henley missing all three
placket buttons. Blues show arriving via radio, volume
goosed maybe a little too high now that I've suddenly
decided to tack on this kwikjyze -- an impulse.)
     Am I happy with the first fictogleanings? No. No
and yes. Some good things here and there: they popped
up almost in spite of myself. Certainly it's always the
best I can do at the moment even though I incorrigibly
believe I ought to be doing a lot better. -- Blazing
away at one in the morning (after a day of all-time
record heat in these parts, I mean the highest
temperature ever recorded, and not just for any
particular date but for all dates; and they say today

may top that) with D asleep and the house quiet, me
authentically fictojyzing for the first time ever, in my
study (at the desk) and thinking of it as the garage
garret in Mentoka Falls, eight p.m. on Tuesday,
September 22, of a year not to be specified (but I do
know it's year 11 on the standard perpetual calendar).

Hard to tell if the fractured approach is working.
So far it hasn't produced anything all that bizarre. I
think it'll happen though. As I get more comfortable
(if I do) strangeness will surely start to creep in.
And beauty and sadness and joy too, let's hope.

Can I also be thoughtful? Speedoo as Mr. Big
Think? Doubts, doubts, but I've got to find a way.
Smuggle in some thought somehow.

One trouble is that at the beginning I, this G,
know way too much and it's tough to keep most of it out
of fictive G's head and yet at the same time let him
think impulsively and act spontaneously. Some of that
I'll have to doctor in on later drafts. If I can.

-- But I don't want to be talking troubles. The
next draft I'll worry about troubles.

This during my second week of vacation for this
year. It'll be interesting to see what it takes to
keep pulling this off when I'm back to working forty
hours a week and commuting close to thirty. And for
that matter what it takes to pull off the next entry in
the orientation chapter later tonight. This is all a
new kind of beginning for me -- feels as if I'm jet-
lagged or something. Where am I? Staggering around.

-- D now moving out of exercise mode. Best I lay
this aside. (Urgent preparations are underway: Mama
and Papa U will soon be descending. Countdown under
ten days -- in fact under nine -- and stress levels are
soaring.)

-- So back to it, Now-Now Land. Fictojyzone, funky
old No. 3 presiding (on a special wooden pedestal I made
for it last week). Just had to slip in this note and
bid "Jyzeburst" (as this volume is now demanding to be
called) a fond adieu.

2.

        Six more days gone by and still thrashing around.
Do I have something or do I not? Certainly it's not
happening as smoothly as I wanted. Not that this is
anything new. It's always a struggle even though
fascinating and in its own way a trip. The process is
fine, yes, and I love being involved in it, wrapped up,
absorbed; it's only the quality of the end product that
causes pain.
        -- Just let loose with whatever pops into the jyze
lobe. Right here and now. Is what I'd like to do
anyway. But not if it's unadulterated gibberish.
Adulterated, well okay. Provisionally I'm saying --
which come to think of it is the only way to go.
        Jyze penchant? Pen chant jyze! Enchant jyze!
        (Maybe I'm just thinking fill up this JB comp book
and then I can more righteously be done with it. Just
thirteen pages to go. Or of course I could razor some
out. -- But I can't resist this one last encore.)
        Right here one of the old red alarm clocks ticks
loudly. This afternoon for the first time ever I tried
using not just one but two of these clocks as noise-
maskers for sleeping. "Red noise." Because one ticked
slightly faster, their ticks would go in and out of sync
-- and in stereo, as it were, with one to either side of
my noggin, on the headboard just above pillow level.
Roughly once every two minutes clock A would lap clock
B, meaning outrun it by a full second. Also for a while
the radio was turned on to static, but I had to give
that up because it started bursting out sporadically
with volleys of loud cracks and pops whenever the fridge
or the septic system switched off or on, say, or D
turned something off or on, or for who knows what other
reason or reasons.
        All this because two "Japan Japanee" relatives of
the several-times-removed type were visiting. (Fine

folks. But I understood at most maybe one of every four
or five words they said and excused myself -- my usual
nightscoper excuse -- after about twenty minutes. -- It
was also a kind of dress rehearsal for the U's visit
starting in just forty-four hours.)

And I should note, or anyway will, that the jays
are very loud these days. Sometimes as many as half a
dozen are flashing around in the vicinity of the feeders
near our bedroom window. They send up an unbelievable
racket, especially when they spot a cat. But after a
while you get used to them. (All graveyard-shift
workers face this problem of keeping things quiet enough
for sleep during the day. We talk about it a lot on the
boats -- that is, when we're not trying to catch up on
our zees on the booth benches.) (These days at home I
use a black washcloth folded into a triangle to cover my
eyes. And also keep a loud fan going. And turn off the
telephone. And I usually sleep pretty good.)

For a week or so what was billed as "the biggest
event in the solar system in all of recorded history"
was going on, a series of comet fragments crashing into
the planet Jupiter. But it wasn't visible to the naked
eye and I never heard anyone utter a single word about
it. I didn't myself. Nor did I see any TV coverage of
it. (What's the point here? Dunno.)

Jazz. Jyze.

-- Also more shrieks in the night. Same boisterous
skinheads on the next street. Loud music. Big parties.
Brawls. One night we wondered if someone was getting
killed up there. Pondered calling the county cops. But
we hesitate to do that because of the high likelihood of
retaliation. A gated suburb this is not. And
eventually things quieted down. The police blotter in
this week's south-county paper showed no incidents in
our area. Several of our neighbors are retired military
and/or current militia members and might -- you never
know -- go after these jokers with guns. Bazookas even.

Right there a fine note to shut down on. Just
keeping a jyze hand in, that's all. The new thought,
though, is I might need this outlet after all. For

purgation maybe. Or could be I'm hooked, yup. On JIRT.
Could be it keeps me sane so I can go berserko on the
JIFT. (And right then, by sheer coincidence, the septic
system shut down. It's another kind of hook I can't
ignore -- not a hook in but a hook out, as in give that
act the hook. Flush it! May it enrich a deserving
drainfield!)

3.

     Some grim news. Or at least likely to turn out
grim, though nothing's certain yet. But it's got me
scrambling already.
     It came in the form of an envelope taped to my
computer screen at work. A kind of Dear John letter
from partner Fran. Or actually it's a warning that such
a letter may soon arrive because a "reduction in force"
will be occurring. The firm will be cutting back --
RIFing -- to just two full-time scopers, perhaps as soon
as two months from now. Doris will be one of the two
kept on. The other's between me and Amy. And for a
host of reasons Amy has the edge. (Thomas is out of the
running. Cathy quit last month and who even knew? She
lasted less than three months.)
     (And why this jyze return to the real? Because it
can't be denied, that's why. Gotta do it: all systems
say so. Also, what matters even more, the jyze gods say
so. Meanwhile work on "Jyzer" will proceed regardless
-- or not. But it's proceeding so far.)
     My next step? I'll try to convince the partners it
would be worth their while to keep me on as a part-time
nightscoper (in addition to the two full-time
dayscopers). That failing, and I judge the chances to
be at least fifty/fifty that it will be doing just that,
I'll have the option of applying for the other day job.
But as of now I doubt I'll do it. If they don't want me
enough to offer me the job outright over Amy I don't

think I want to be working for them anymore. "I would prefer not to." -- And especially not as a dayscoper forced to put up with all the hassles of rush-hour commuting, dressing up (rather than down), trying to get along with the rest of the day crew (even absent Amy) (and I know about this because I've worked a few shifts -- twice a whole week straight -- on daytime relief).

Sad. But I understand why they feel as they do. Technological advances are putting the squeeze on the court-reporting vocation as a whole and making scopers obsolete. I'm "overqualified" for the job and it's hard for them to understand what I'm all about. They'd rather deal with someone who's more like them, even if she's an extremely ornery person (as everyone says Amy is) who's much less skilled as a scoper (and Fran's letter comes right out and says this).

So it goes. By and large I've known all the above for a long time. It's actually more surprising to me that it's taken this long for it to happen: the blade to fall.

Yet this job is so close to ideal for me in its present nightscoper form that I'll see if I can slip a good-size rock between the blade and the block and save my neck for a while longer. It's worth the effort. And I know I have some allies in the firm (especially Naomi and Verna, the reporters whose work I scope most often) and I'll ask them to try to talk the partners into keeping me on as a part-time nightscoper handling government work and overnight rush jobs and overflow during busy periods -- which is essentially what I was doing for my first five years with the firm.

-- If the rock (mentioned above) shatters the blade, I'll be delighted. As always I'd much prefer working maybe fifteen hours a week. It would involve some belt-tightening at home but the free time is just what I need, now more than ever. (If they say they'll go along with this but also insist that I take a pay cut, then I'll have to do some hard thinking.)

And if blade shatters rock? If they can't offer me any guaranteed hours at all? Then the big scramble begins. It's not too likely I'll be able to find another job anywhere near as good in terms of either pay or benefits or working conditions or perks (especially the sanctioned use of office computers and printers for my own work). In fact it's highly improbable I could find a job as good in any one of these respects, let alone all at once. Chances are I'd have to take a scuzz job (maybe after a spell on unemployment) and ask D to do the same.

Or we could move to D's home turf. Sell the property here and take up her parents' standing offer to put us up over there, either at their house or in a nearby apartment building they're part-owners of. This would still involve my finding a job, but I'd probably have a better chance of turning up something half-decent there through the U family's connections.

The main hang-up here is D's longstanding reluctance to make such a move. It could put a lot of strain on our relationship. She doubts I'd be able to bear up under all the requisite old-country-style family obligations over the long haul, and she could be right. But when we moved to our current abode we talked about staying there for five years and then moving to be near her parents. Five years is almost up. Her parents are now at the stage where she feels they need her, their only child, to be nearby, at least as she projected things out a few years back. I long ago agreed to go with her when she felt it was time.

The four of us have already talked this over (the U's arrived Friday night). The others don't know yet just how dire my work crisis probably is, but I've told them all it's quite clear the firm's need for a nightscoper is declining and I could be out of a job before much longer, maybe even in the next few months (no need to get D alarmed about all this until I know whether the firm will accept my proposal for a part-time nightscoper position). But the U's' offer to put us up with them still stands. They'll also start scouting for possible job openings for me over there.

-- Because of this fallback option I'm not really

peering into the abyss. Therefore I can deal with the
RIF crisis with a fair amount of equanimity (though the
first few hours were pretty grim regardless). But I
don't like having the distractions interfering with my
own personal work, and of course those distractions
could soon be a lot worse if I'm entirely out of a job.
Looking for another job, preparing the house and
property for sale, packing, applying for unemployment --
all kinds of unsavory prospects.

     -- Right now I'm holed up at the train station in
the city and I'm here in part because of one of those
distractions. I have all my writings and a huge mass of
research notes stored on backup disks keyed to the
office computer system -- altogether more than a hundred
disks -- and in the weeks ahead I'll have to copy all
of them over to a universal type of program called
ASCII. This won't be difficult but it will involve a
lot of time-consuming labor (all of the headers have to
be taken out individually, for example) and everything
will have to be done on the sly. Therefore I'm planning
to go in at least one extra night a week, and in fact
that's what I'm doing right now.

     It's Sunday night and with an exception or two I
haven't worked a Sunday night in years. It won't be all
that terrible if someone finds me there when ordinarily
I shouldn't be (I do have other "legitimate" work I can
pretend to be dealing with) but I'd prefer it not to
happen. I'm a little worried they'll be thinking I'm
angry over these recent developments and might be
wanting to retaliate (say by wiping out a few reporters'
transcription dictionaries) and therefore maybe they'd
better boot me out right now -- before I can get my
disks copied. And that could cost me a great deal of
time and expense later on. And so to reduce the chances
of being discovered at the office when I'm not supposed
to be there I'm scheming to show up fairly late, say
about eleven. Which means I still have about an hour to
kill.

     And five pages to go before this volume is full.
How handy it is that I get to close it out with a little

drama (and never mind how prosaically I'm treating it so
far), and especially this particular job-loss drama,
which happens to be quite similar to the one I was
facing back at Mezzu along about late February of my
first year there -- which just happens to be quite close
to the time this journal entry here just might be used
as a model of sorts for "Jyzer," because fictive G will
be facing that same kind of crisis.

    And speaking of "Jyzer," how's it doing? Can't
say. And shouldn't say. That's what I'm thinking now.
Concentrate right here. -- What I mean is I don't know
anything about "Jyzer" I didn't know before. But I'm
continuing on schedule so far and that's all I want to
note. Just keep grinding it out. This jyze here,
meanwhile, I think, ought to be focusing on something
else. After all, until recently I was planning to give
it up entirely until the "Jyzer" draft was finished.
And now with the job crisis, it -- this JIRT --
definitely has something else to focus on. In this
sense one might even say the crisis has its good side.

    Meanwhile the freights keep rolling through. At
first the big waiting room was almost empty -- just me
and one other guy reading a newspaper. But it's
gradually filling up, and most of the people here -- I
may be the only exception -- are present to meet trains
that are running late. Or very late. Or ridiculously
late. I'm sitting right by the board and everyone comes
over here first to see when their train is due in. Then
they give out a small, a medium, or a large groan.

    Anything else? Yes. A surprise call at five a.m.
this week at the office. Jang. Just to let me know
Elgie's now in school in Seoul. This was almost a shock
because it was the first time in years she's felt the
need or even been willing to update me on his doings.
Unfortunately I was busy at the time and my deadline to
make a dash for the ferry was fast approaching; I
couldn't talk more than a minute or two. But yes, this
is the same woman I'm writing about in "Jyzer": Lady S.
Sounds the same too. In a word: not real happy with me.
Meaning what at this point, if anything, I have no idea.

[A Jyze Swerve]

     -- Twenty after eleven says the big wall clock.
Security guy with a walkie-talkie strolling through.
And an update on the last of today's scheduled
continentals: its new arrival time is 1:30 a.m. (Train
whistle, rumble of a freight, floor vibrating although
only slightly -- which likely means the freight's
deadheading down to the docks.)
     Maybe I'll just mosey on up to the office now
and finish off this J-book later. Only one two-sided
page to go before I hit the notes coming back this
way.
     -- Or yeah, probably better, strop up the razor
to cut out those two pages. Make ready for JB No. 2,
identical with the green "Jyzer" J-books except the
cover is black.
     If my health holds up: always that "if." Lose my
job? who cares! Forward! Inward! Outward! Wherever!
(And if I survive this late hike through the mean
streets.)

BOOK II

CHAPTER FIVE

[Jyzelby the Scoper]

1.

    The height of summer. Down below, the six-twenty
(running forty minutes late) is packed to the gunwales,
mostly with RVs. Up here loads of folks are wandering
about in shorts and bathing suits and letting fly with
excited queries such as "Look, is that a submarine?" and
"Where's the ship that started the Vietnam War?" Old
Glory snaps smartly in numerous places within view
outside. All doors are wide open and the usual flock of
panhandling pigeons is strolling about inside the cabin
cooing out their pitches and pleas.
    And jyze is going down here because this very
afternoon the voice on high spoke to me yet once again
in the shower: "For the good of jyze as a whole, Jyzer
G," it said, "you must keep the JIRT jyze flowing no
matter what." And so I intend to do just that on a
regular basis -- like once a week if possible -- until
this new, much thicker volume is a wrap.
    (Water so blue out there. Glint and glare. Just
about everyone in here wearing shades, me included.
-- And it's a bumper tourist season. In these parts,
that is. Highly publicized mayhem committed upon
tourists in other "major U.S. destinations" earlier this
year likely has much to do with this. Of course it's
just a matter of time until similar horrors manifest
here. Or maybe they're already doing so and we're
better at keeping them quiet.)
    And the RIF crisis? It continues. This is Sunday

(again) and just as last Sunday I'm bound for the
office, my mission this time to punch in some
corrections and do some typing. Decided I might as
well correct the typos and print clean copies of
certain old writings of mine (protojyze mostly) before
redoing the storage disks for them (though I redid them
once already, last week). This'll amount to maybe a
few hundred pages, for which I'll be using the office
printers, which are so much faster and better than my
own printer at home. But then again I'll be supplying
the toner and paper, so my personal work won't be
costing the firm anything (their printers, churning out
upwards of 25K pages a week, are on a maintenance
contract that covers everything; mine isn't). And I'm
officially sanctioned to use the machines for my own
stuff anyway. It's just that I doubt the partners ever
imagined I'd be printing this many pages at a pop.

But no, no more on that. Not right now. I'll try
to spread out all this job-crisis stuff. RIF, RIF! Try
not to obsess on it, though I'll probably obsess anyway.

-- About here on Friday evening we came upon a pod
of orcas. Highly unusual this far south in the sound.
It created a sensation, scores of folks dashing to the
bow rail and then back to the stern when the pod popped
up again behind us. No more than the train depot last
week did the boat tip or tilt, but it too seemed it
should. Glistening black-and-white beasts gorgeous to
behold, splashing about like porpoises but without that
crass porpoisian catering for approval (even though in
actuality they are porpoises). "Them dudes are baaaad!"

-- And here comes the city. Usual skyline compleat
with usual icons. All camcorders to the front, please.
Sleeking by yachtlike, a gleaming white Coast Guard
cutter with a nifty diagonal red slash painted parallel
to the prow line. Clunking by, a tugboat hauling two
beater barges (but my view's suddenly blocked by a very
large woman in chartreuse bermudas pushing a mammoth
baby carriage, probably packing twins or maybe even
triplets). -- And a grunge guy sprawled in the booth to
my right, he's impressively disdainful of it all.

[Jyzelby the Scoper]

     Now a view of the cruise ship that ran aground last
week and limped back to port: it's lifted high in dry
dock like a wheelless car on cinderbricks. And here's
another set of barges, this one stacked with yellow
containers rising well above the level of our deck and
being pulled by a ludicrously tiny tug -- recalls those
colossal loads riding the backs of bicycles in a distant
city in a long-gone era. (And still today in that city?
Maybe a few. -- Same city, I'll note, Lady S called me
from week before last.)
     Hey: the grunge guy's a phony! A weekend grungie!
He's reading a biology text and wielding a yellow
highlighter! -- But in character he's a mean actor in
at least two senses of that term. I was totally fooled.
Break a leg, punk!
     Great gray blister of the domed stadium dead ahead
-- shut down at the moment because tiles have been
falling from the ceiling. A big scandal over this, but
muted now with the national pastime out on strike (for
real!).
     I won't ask myself if this entry rises to true jyze
standards. (There's the brick clock tower of the
railroad depot; it sticks out like an intruder from
nineteenth-century Italy, I'll say.) -- My excuse is
it's still not established once and for all what those
jyze standards are. (Not really: and regardless they'll
never be all that confining anyway or I might as well
hang it up right now.)
     -- And I haven't decided yet where to hunker down
while awaiting the optimal hour to ascend to the office.
-- But we're in (with a bigger THUNK than usual).
                    *   *
     Stood on the cityside third-story deck of the state
ferry terminal mulling my options. Down below,
pedestrian crowds streaming by, a white horse-drawn
carriage clip-clopping by, a green-and-cream waterfront
streetcar rattling by (with a startlingly loud toot on
its steam whistle). On the old dirty-gray double-deck
viaduct directly across the street and on the four-lane
boulevard down below, cars whizzing by. On the breeze

the aroma of smoked salmon wafting in. On the
lightpoles colorful windsock banners rippling raucously.
And I thought: hm, not many options really, especially
considering that I'm carrying, along with my usual
backpack, a small suitcase (once Lady S's) containing
the printing supplies and various protojyze segments
I'll be typing up. Maybe I'll just go back inside.

So it's the Slip 2 waiting room. My monthly pass
gets me in here anytime, even if I've just left, as now.
Other than the railroad depot and the office itself,
this is the only place in the easily walkable part of
downtown where I can hang out indoors after dark without
having to buy something.

Highbacked wooden benches in here. Vending
machines and linoleum floors. Not too much interior
atmosphere. All-glass twelve-foot-high wall, though,
lightly tinted, facing south: good third-story view of
the working waterfront. Similar glass wall straight
ahead, but the view there is mostly blocked by the
loading ramp. Destination signs glowing in orange neon.
Pink sunset rays lasering through in scattered places.

Meanwhile the waiting areas for both slips are
filling up. About ten minutes until the next boat's due
in at Slip 1. Splash of cards being shuffled, clunk of
cans landing in vending-machine ports, pop-and-hiss of
those same cans being opened. An unfamiliar foreign
language being spoken nearby -- definitely not Jyzese.

Sunset's just about over. Waterfront sights fade
as interior window reflections vivify (there he is
again, the jyzer hard at it!). Kids racing around
nearby making lots of racket: I wouldn't be surprised if
the scruffy drunk sprawled out on the next bench took a
swipe at them. And if he doesn't, I might.

Here it comes, the boat pulling in. (And he's up,
the drunk, coughs and mutters aloud to himself,
"Standing back up almost ain't worth it." And off he
staggers to the gate.) (Pilothouse of the arriving
ferry silhouetted picturesquely against darkening pink
above the mountains. Can almost make out in the
pilothouse window -- but can't, except as a kind of

[Jyzelby the Scoper]

stereotype projection from my own private stock of
nautical images -- almost make out a captain silhouette
complete with captain's cap and beard and pipe.)
     As for the RIF crisis, it's like this. I waited a
couple of days and wrote partner Fran a one-page memo
asking for clarification on certain matters in her
letter. Is she ruling out hiring me part-time for night
work with guaranteed hours, say fifteen a week? Would
it be possible to go with an arrangement like that on a
trial basis before taking more extreme steps? She
didn't come in to the office for a couple of days and so
didn't get the memo until Friday. I didn't find a reply
awaiting me Friday night, so I figure she's thinking on
it -- probably talking it over with partner Una. That
she didn't reject it out of hand is a good sign; the
odds for a tolerable outcome improve a little.
     This week should tell the story. If the partners
won't guarantee part-time night hours I'll ask the
reporters I'm closest to (my two champions) to urge
them, the partners, to reconsider. If that fails I'll
see if I can work something out with those same two
reporters where I'd scope for them privately on a
piecework basis, per page or per word. If that also
fails, I'm out. RIF'd. Eighty-sixed. Scuttled.
     -- Meanwhile the nine o'clock has unloaded and
reloaded. A few stragglers are trotting through the
near-empty waiting room (as I've done many a time
myself) in hopes of reaching the ramp before the gate
closes. Scarcely any color at all left in the nimbus of
darkening gray out there, more like an airborne
scattering of faintly pink dust. Also a couple of
horizontally elongated inky-black brushstroke clouds
have drifted in low enough and close enough to appear to
be impaled on the highest peaks.
     "Last call, last call." Pounding feet. "Wait!"
Panting. "Wait! Wait!" And there he goes. He made
it. In a suit, no less, with a fancy laptop pack
flopping around on his back and a hand awkwardly
reaching around to steady it. The gate clangs behind
him with shuddery metallic finality.

-- And how's the redoubtable "Jyzer," i.e. the book itself, doing? Forget it. Last night's planned session had to be scratched, as in canceled. When not brooding over my job future I'm required to be amiably conversational with the U's, who after all are likable folks and laboring hard to shape up the property (entirely understandable since, as perhaps not noted earlier, it's theirs and they're planning to sell it before much longer). Along the way they're tending to lots of caretaking tasks which I should be doing myself and would be doing if I didn't have this longstanding arrangement with D under which she's supposed to be doing them -- at her own insistence! -- while I bring home the bacon; and she does try to do them but even when her health's good she's really not cut out for some of them -- many of them -- and of course she's lazy too in certain areas, just like me -- housework and yard work topping the "shirk" list for both of us.

Sunset all gone. Another big boat (super-jumbo class) has glided into Slip 2 while my attention's been elsewhere. Bells going off, clatter of vehicles disembarking as if they're bouncing over loose planks, which in fact they're very likely doing. I'm thinking I'll risk an earlier arrival at the office tonight. Let's say ten o'clock. Chances of running into a reporter are slim. And even if I did, the odds of anyone objecting to what I'm up to or even taking the slightest notice of it are slimmer still. I'm just trying to play it maximally safe, that's all.

-- Not that I'm bailing on "Jyzer." No way. I'll just have to ride out this interruption. Sometimes there's nothing you can do but suspend everything. With only the U's' visit or only the RIF crisis I would've been able to keep charging ahead but not with both.

So it is. And onward. To the office ho.

[Jyzelby the Scoper]

2.

    Can't take any more of this guy. He's a snob and a
crank -- pompous, didactic, bitter -- insufferable.
I've seen him that way all along but I wanted to try him
again, thinking maybe the distortions of the age (or my
age when I first read him) had caused me to miss
something important. But now I find him even more
objectionable. And I'm only on page seventeen of this
miserable tome for which I laid out almost thirty bucks.
    Meanwhile (as the ferry labors eastward, again a
six-twenty on a Sunday but today's overcast and chilly
for August, and consequently the voyage is a whole
different kind) -- meanwhile, I say, the RIF crisis
is still closing in, the pressure having ratcheted up
by (to ballpark it) an order of magnitude or so.
    It was almost two orders. For a couple of days it
appeared the U's had decided to put U Acres (as we're
all calling it now) on the market immediately, meaning D
and I would have to start grappling with all the (may I
say hassles? ordeals?) -- and I mean right now:
packing, spiffing up the house and grounds, looking for
a new place, the whole nine yards or rather one very big
landscaped yard plus two acres of wetland (because D's
not ready just yet, she's now let me know -- in no
uncertain terms -- for us to go back where she came from
and try living there). Mama U was especially hot for
this sell-it-now idea, maybe because she'd like to have
us domiciled nearby -- and in the same house if possible
-- to help keep Papa U's tyrant tendencies in check.
And maybe for some other reasons too. But Papa U wasn't
going for it, thank the gods. We've been granted an
extension until next year, maybe even a year beyond
that. So at least we'll have a roof over our heads.
    Beyond that, who knows. Partner Fran rejected my
offer to keep working nights part-time. Her "letter of
clarification" was indeed very clear. In several places

what I regard as a wholly unjustified hostile tone crept
in -- not for the first time in our dealings, though by
and large she's always been fair enough with me and
usually quite friendly -- and so now I'm thinking I
might do better to aim my appeal more toward partner
Una. I do have a strategy and new proposals to make.
If these fail (there are two, and both long shots) I'll
approach the reporters individually with the
independent-contractor idea noted in these pages last
week. If they go for it, I'll offer the firm some
incentives to keep making its machines available to me
even though my pay would be coming directly from the
individual reporters. (It's too complex to explain
beyond that. It's not a bad scheme -- offers a little
something for everybody -- and it just might work.)
     After that, if they don't go for that one either, a
flyer to every reporter firm in the area. "Experienced
nightscoper available." We see a blizzard of these
flyers every week at the office, but they rarely say
"night" before "scoper"; that might be my salvation.
It's the one trick that separates me from the other
ponies. It's worked before and it might be good for one
last whinny. Or nicker maybe.   Or snicker, right.
     -- And that's it for the ride in. (All this
sounding so blase or something, nonchalant, I don't
know, cavalier even, but I've been worrying a lot, to
the exclusion of just about everything else, including
sleep. Until I figure out how to proceed I worry things
incessantly. For a few days I thought I had stumbled
upon a workable path forward but then this house-sale
business came up.)

*   *

     -- No telling how long I'll be able to hang on
here. A fountain ledge at the new "staircase park," as
it's called, what's really just a street-wide outdoor
hillside set of steps with a few small fountains and
waterfalls and planters containing tiny designer trees
built into it, one block long, right on one of my
standard routes to the office.
     Presumably installing this "park" was a way the

68

developer could legally tack a few extra stories onto
the spiffy new highrise that's gone up right next to it.
And the trade-off's working passably well, I'd say,
considering the likely alternatives. Just opened last
week. A few tourists poking around at the moment but a
few crazies too, including a big fireburst-hair guy who
stopped by to jab a finger over and over, daggerlike,
into the small rectangular pool five or six feet to my
right, muttering maniacally as he did so. Flying high
maybe but more likely demented or possibly both. Made
some impressive splashes too. And despite his crazed
state he took care not to aim those splashes at me and
I appreciated that. (Another street dude maybe twenty
steps down just unleashed a Tarzan cry. It set off a
surprisingly complex echo.)

What was happening back there on the ferry, I was
trying to read a certain cranky poet's published journal
but finally gave it up in disgust and decided to write
some of my own nonsense. "Jyze," a voice said, as in
"Drive, He Said." So I'm jyzing.

Waterfront a block away. Just about sunset. On
this side of the pond it's a little warmer and only
about two-thirds overcast. As dark comes on, the neon
sign on the pier straight down the street glows redder
by the minute. The breeze off the water is frisky
enough that I get hit occasionally by liquid splinters
from the fountains down below. (The fountain for this
pool I'm sitting next to is out of order -- already.
And it probably won't be long before the whole park
is. Although in theory the concrete stairs should be
good for a while.)

-- A couple of blocks north a summer concert is
cranking up at one of the piers. Last summer my pal Tom
T. and I ambled down that way several times to listen
knothole-style from outside the high fence. (Tom also
let me observe him up close for "Jyzer" research
purposes as he performed his job as a railroad night
dispatcher.) (Flashbulbs popping here. Slinky female
models suddenly posing one patio level down on the steps
for some sort of fashion shoot. For a moment the

photographer seemed to be gazing straight at me as he
conferred with an assistant and I was sure I was about
to be called on to chip in some local color. So then
more or less by instinct I came up with a bad-ass frown
which by all rights should've been just what he was
looking for. But it wasn't. Maybe it seemed too stagy?
In any case they passed me by. In fact they've trouped
off somewhere else out of sight down below.)

   Dark gray now hereabouts and getting darker and
colder. On the other side sunset's much like last
week's: a narrow band of dusty pink, inky low brushwork
clouds, silhouetted mountain peaks. (Already by page
seventeen the aforementioned poet's journal was making
me skip ahead with its labored sunset descriptions so I
can imagine how mine would be going over if this were
ever offered to the public, even at remainder-table
paperback prices -- as, say, "Authentic Cut-rate Jyze.")
                *   *
   The old broiler. Same one. The joint ain't
changed one lick. Except maybe it's a little more
popular now. With the dive a few blocks to the north
closed permanently it's become downtown's premier
gritty-level 24/7 hangout.

   (Ordering now, the old Nightscoper Special, as I've
dubbed it, a meaty breakfast available at all hours.)

   I've got a window booth. Twin gargantuan thimbles
of a highrise hotel looming out there a short block to
the east, stripped-down urban convenience store
squatting directly across the street. Lots of cops
lurking about, in cruisers and on bikes and on foot.
More than ever these days the really nasty street
action's down in this part of town. But I'm here less
than ever because I come in from the southwest and this
joint's four or five long blocks north of the office.

   (Annoying male-female argument in the booth at my
back: "You blocked me." "I did not block you." On and
on in variations, though slight, on that same theme,
with gradually rising edge and loudness, yet it's still
all in intense whispers. -- And a gleaming white
stretch limo slowly slides by outside for what seems way

too long a time, like a slick special-effects trick.)

Meanwhile I'm ready to do another big batch of surreptitious printing and typing. Last week turned out well and I still have plenty of toner left in the cartridge and two more reams of paper, so why not. No sign anyone's hip to my scam. And if anyone were, why would she care (all are shes at the firm except me and Thomas, and he likes to dress as a she, even at work sometimes). -- And if I'm lucky I'll get the whole final year of protojyze (the spree) typed up before they usher me out the door for the last time -- if that's how it all shakes out.

-- And here it is at last, the platter. (And flashing police lights outside, and the mysterious argument at my back heating up beyond whispers -- it's funny too -- but to hell with that, I'm famished.)

*

And now finished. Good. Lots of grease: I just sliced a few days or possibly weeks off my life. Forbidden pleasure. "Never more than once a month."

What a couple of fighting cocks these two behind me are. A moment ago I hit the men's room just so I could scope them out. He's brown, bald, short, pot-bellied, impeccably suit-and-tied; she's pink, tall, skinny, probably a bit older, flamingly red-haired, dressed like a flapper in seedy purple velvet. Bizarre. And a beautiful little mixed-race girl ("mixusan"?) maybe ten years old is sitting with them, on the man's side of the booth. She looks utterly bored. The rest of us in this area are hanging on every word.

More than half my working life now I've been dropping by this broiler. I still like it a lot. (A pair of sleazo extreme dude-speakers just slid into the booth across from me. -- And one just ripped off one of the brown vinyl seat-cover patches, both literally and figuratively! Stuffed it in his pocket! Is he adding to a collection or what? Working on a "funky found art" project maybe? -- But really, how tacky can you get?)

Friday I took a late ferry home and happened to walk right by cousin Kar as he came ashore with the

chichi suburban-island crowd. Fortunately he was
talking with someone and didn't see me, or otherwise
another social obligation would likely be penciled in
for this weekend on top of the extended one already
scheduled with the U's (poor Kar is desperately seeking
diversions for his visiting kids). And -- in other news
(oops, an ambulance hurtles by, piercing siren) (now
stops in the next block, far side, crowd gathering) --
our new VCR arrived, a snazzy one, our combined birthday
present from the U's. Alas, we have only one video
(obtained by D for free through a promotion) and lacking
credit cards we'll probably be unable to rent any.

And I finished another book on Wachute history.
Came across one ancestral mention, in Gram S's line, and
that just a squib. Apparently they weren't quite the
local movers and shakers I'd been led to picture them
as. Second tier maybe. To make first tier you probably
had to be a mayor or a mogul. My great-grandfather in
that line was almost a mogul (in hardware) but probably
not quite, even by modest local standards. An oil
portrait making him look like Pecos Pete with his locks
partially shorn sits in a box atop the shed loft.

It's almost ten-thirty. Better push on.
(Ambulance and cop-car lights still flashing up the
street but I'm going the other way.)

3.

At a burger joint north of downtown. Bagga grease
with a few molecules of meat and potatoes mixed in right
here to J-book's left, also a large soft-drink cup into
whose X-slitted plastic lid I just plunged a straw.
Sugary poison in there, chosen by me. Choose yours!

Out the window, flashing marquees of a video store
and a cinema (shameless blockbuster schlock playing).
Outdoor tables at the espresso next to the theater
overflowing with boulevardiers almost into the gutter;

otherwise I might be sitting over there myself.

Probably fifty or sixty tables and booths in here but only four occupied. High ceiling. Browns and oranges. Serious plastic but peace and quiet. "A good jyze room." This local chain always wins the laurels for best fries in town and always makes the Top Ten Hangouts list. (So where is everybody?)

Nowadays I get up this way two or three times a year max. Usually my mission is to trade in a birthday or Christmas gift certificate laid on me by brother Rob, sometimes many months before. Trade it in for books, I mean. Trouble is his outfit's good at albums but not so good at books, which is why I procrastinate on coming up here. Never know what I might be able to find. But always do find something.

-- Where things stand on the RIF, I'm waiting for a reply from the reporters. Do any of them want to hire me privately? No big deal if they don't, I said in person to one (stiff upper lip) when she happened in early one morning, just hate to break up a winning team (wink wink). Unless the time has come, that is. And let's face it, maybe it has. (None of them are even close to being boat-rockers.)

Decided to skip making a second appeal to partner Fran. Too much hostility there right now. Better to see first if I have any bargaining power. Leverage. Only through the individual reporters could I have that. Will my years of going the extra mile for them pay off? -- Probably not. But we'll see. In optimistic moments I judge the chances as maybe one in three.

On the home front, the current idea is to put U Acres on the market next spring or summer. If I can't come up with a scoping job (or keep at least a portion of the one I've got) we'll just about have to do that. If I can find a way to hang in there breadwinner-wise, we may be able to talk the U's into letting us stay on at the house one more year beyond next spring.

So everything depends. All's dangling. Suspense. Mystery. And for me it's hard to think about anything else. Obsessive internal monologues and dialogues.

Imaginary ripostes. Duels. Withering scorn. Just
can't help it. But I do manage to keep most of it to
myself. The important thing, the only thing, is landing
on my feet. It will do no good at all to "prove" what a
blithering idiot Fran is being about all this, either to
Fran herself or to anyone else.

    -- And so it goes. I'm again on the way in for a
round of typing, edit-punching, and printing clean
copies of my own work, pretty much the same as the past
few Sundays. Things could drag on like this for several
more weeks or even months (if business should happen to
pick up at the office, as it often does in the fall).
Or things could come to a head at any moment. The firm
itself could go down in flames. My luring a reporter or
two off the office scoping system could be the final
straw or the incendiary's match (and given the cool
treatment I've been getting from the firm in recent
times I would not weep if it were).

    Traffic rolling by. Bright neon colors. After
shopping for books I'll catch a bus back in. Downtown's
easy walking distance but at night the walk's far too
perilous for me or anyone else not packing heat (as I
believe they still say). Yet this is just the same old
city, so familiar to me it's hard to believe it could be
a mortal threat to anyone. As I sit here now its feel-
good icon looms right behind me like a giant neon golf
tee. (And beneath it the old coliseum gapes in a state
of near-maximal disassembly, just its main beams still
standing -- like a massive yurt frame spanning the top
of a huge pit -- as it undergoes renovation.)

    (Any thoughts about the cataclysmic events of
twelve years ago in this hood, the ones involving Lady U
the dancing dervish and Marco R. the devilishly handsome
leading man from the far coast? None to speak of.
Other things on my mind right now.)

    -- Rob's visiting Mother this week, though I know
this only because a postcard from her said so. And last
night we threw a birthday party for Mama U. "Caution:
Party Zone." Pumped up the balloon crowd for another
round and added a few new faces. High hilarity reigned

at the old homestead. (Mama U promised me a crack later
at the book I gave her, "when you're living with us.")

4.

    Birthday morning, my own. A rustic wooden bench on
the waterfront boardwalk at the home port. Such a fine
blue morning it is -- as now one of the foot ferries
backs out from the dock, pivots, roars off toward the
state dock a mile across the inlet -- same boat I just
rode from there to here. The only one in the fleet
that's younger than I am. Big V wake. Otherwise the
water is mirrory calm.
    Bring to this an attitude. Some acidic vigor. Or
try anyway, probably only to fail because I'm too worn
down by a hard night at the screens. "Brain fried."
Hadn't noticed this before, but my reactions are
sluggish and it only stands to reason that's why.
    Two of the three remaining dayscopers left me
birthday cards. Nippers and Turkey. For Nippers (Amy)
this is a first: I suspect she's mainly trying to look
good for the partners. Turkey (Doris), her message is
unexpectedly somber and says she hopes the coming year
is better for me than this past year. Sure she does!
Turkey the confessed saboteur of several of my jobs a
few years back (from sheer scope-envy, as the partners
surmised before tapping her on the wrist for it). And
besides, what's she talking about? This past year's
been terrific for me! Turkey my buddy who still hasn't
said a single word to me about the RIF. Turkey whose
sucking up to the newly stern Master in Chancery
herself, partner Fran, has paid off, I guess, if being
chosen to continue working days in that hellhole (with
Nippers! with the Master!) can be called a payoff.
    In case it's not obvious from the names, I reread
my favorite scrivener's tale the other night. RIFs
through the ages. To this latter-day Jyzelby right here

the parallels were astounding.

I wouldn't deny I'm bitter. These creeps. But then it's what happens when you refuse to play their games. And more and more over the past several years I've been refusing. So now I get to pay the piper. Just how it is and I'm not trying to pretend otherwise.

No word yet from reporter Naomi. Turned out she was out of town over the weekend, didn't get my note until yesterday.

-- The foot ferry has landed, across the inlet at the state dock. Hard by the huge shipyard crane. In fact it's already taken off again and is plowing back this way. -- Long line of gray U.S. Navy ships over there, active type to the near left and mothballed to the far left. Jagged mountain peaks up close behind all of them and to the south. Thickets of sailboat masts here in the foreground and all standing stock still again after their mass-metronoming caused by the waves hitting from the foot ferry when it first pulled out. The rest of the foot-ferry fleet quietly hugging their docks. All but one (more a tour boat) I ride regularly. Usually in the evening I'm aboard the oldest of the lot, the "floating museum," a handsome wooden double-decker christened in the year of my father's birth.

Soon I have to put a lid on it and make for the bus stop half a block up the boardwalk. Only a couple of dozen days a year at most is it warm and dry enough for me to sit out here during my morning layover. Today the sun's just a few degrees above the horizon, the bench damp, the breeze chilly. This may be my last time this year -- or ever. (No boo-hoos. "Just how it is" -- now elevated to a jyze catchphrase.)

Diver birds exert a fascination. They go down, you wonder where and when they'll pop back up. Sometimes it seems they don't. (But surely they almost always do. Out of sight on the far side of the docked ferries, most likely. It's a real long shot that a sea lion would be lurking down there to gobble them up.)

-- Here it is, the foot ferry angling in. And I'm hightailing it busward. The bus (mini size, more like a

van) takes off as soon as the passengers from this ferry
board. An hour until the next one.

*   *

      Just took a whiz back behind the shed. Now sitting
on the front threshold and with the door swung fully out
and hooked in place flat against the siding I can gaze
upon all that's beholdable and say it's one atrociously
gorgeous day. Lawn neatly cut, trees and bushes freshly
trimmed, sky a gaspingly fresh blue. Shadow of a skinny
basketball-hoop-high Japanese maple stretching three
times its height left to right on the grass (that's
downhill; everything out here is downhill left to right,
east to west; could even say everything's downhill,
period, these days -- but must resist).
      Birds cheep-cheep-cheep. Or I forgot, make that
Jeep-Jeep-Jeep. It's Jyzeman Jeep, he's at it again.
-- This Jeep is a nickname that's actually legit,
bestowed on me, and thus on fictive narrator G, though
of course the bestower didn't know that latter part of
it, by Gramps S of Mentoka provenance. What's more it
can legitimately be lowercased, as the word jeep itself
was when it first emerged as a workaday acronym for
General Purpose, G.P., back before the auto companies,
or one of them anyway, usurped the name. (Why did I let
this excellent nickname languish so long? Instead
around age ten I launched a campaign for Spike which
never did catch on. After that, back to the default
Sandy. -- That's outside the family only. If it were
inside, confusion would rein since we're all Sandys.)
      As I left the house D was putting in a call to the
power company: the juice is out again. Happens a couple
of times a month around here. With so many trees and
such feeble root systems, so much rainfall and such
ungrasping soil, everything's at the wind's mercy. We
no longer bother to report an outage until at least
three hours go by. In this part of the region you could
almost define how backwoods you are by the number of
hours you routinely wait before making that call.
      Her parents got off safely this morning but not
uneventfully: just before leaving they learned by phone

77

that their house had been burgled. At least one large
prizewinning bonsai plant was missing. ("But," as D
filled me in, "they don't really like that one anyway.")
     -- Now I should kick back or anyway lean back and
think, really think. About, for instance, the meaning
of all this. This marker of a day, I'm saying. (Forget
bonsai burglars, for now anyway, since my next job may
well be guarding against them.) On a birthday you can't
help it, you want meaning. You want portents. You're
"older and wiser" and therefore you'd like to come up
with something to show that the more flattering of those
terms really does apply. (It does occur to me it would
be wise not to sit here where the deer ticks can get at
me -- pump me full of Lyme disease, which I suppose
might be called the virtuous backwoods zen-hubby's
version of AIDS. -- And mixed in with all the morning
sweetness in the air from flowers and earth and green
things, the unmistakable acrid tinge of deer piss and
maybe human too, namely my own, from the community piss
patch in the bushes just the other side of the shed.
Right where, in fact, the wetland officially begins.)
     Age. Too bad this cedar siding here on the shed
isn't aging more gracefully. Owing to the protective
coating I misguidedly brushed on it it's going vintage
in dismayingly uneven fashion. Like me? Maybe so.
(Thinking the last time I sat on a shed threshold -- as
now I slide with relief to the ground and use the shed
floor, about eight inches above ground level, as a
jyzing platform -- the last time was back at our second
city rental house in the month of the raging hornets
during the year of the last and final protojyze spree.)
     The ephemerality of it all. Wasn't it just a few
weeks ago I was gushing about how I deserved all this
idyllic splendor? The idyl now shattered! Almost!
What payback, what cosmic justice and so swift! -- But
no, I didn't really mean it that seemingly hubristic way
back then. I was just amazed I'd been granted even
temporary access to something so paradisiacal. Same for
my nightscoping job: far better luck there than I ever
dreamed of. To be bitter over the impending loss is

just a dumb knee-jerk thing, as in wounded vanity.
What, they would RIF a fine fellow like me? (But later
on when I'm slogging away at something far worse or
half-starving I may not be so quick to strike this pose.
-- Yeah, it's a pose too, even if felt.) (And it is
felt.)
     So take that, Hugh Briss.
     -- Feet crossed in the grass. Mostly brown grass
in this area. Large swatches of the lawn in fact. A
dry summer. Not really all that idyllic after all,
though still good for the chief in-house mow-person
since so much less mowing is required. (Horse whinnies.
Small plane drones overhead, probably feds sniffing out
meth labs or marijuana grows. And I'd better be signing
off soon, being uncomfortable in this position, and it's
late anyway, and I need sleep, and after reading a
certain modern-day cynic I think my god I'm lucky I
still can sleep at all -- or was it his insomnia that,
as the cynic himself likes to say, was the source of
everything he later wrote, and would something like that
maybe work for me too? No, I don't think so. -- This
being the reigning fad catchphrase culturewide: "I don't
think so." Like "make my day" or "read my lips" and a
thousand others inflated from respectably workable
cliches and now fallen on hard times, all but
unspeakable. In the long run of course it's hard to
think of a phrase that doesn't fall into that category.
Except for: jyze on, fool!)
     -- Back later. In the old tradition. Resurrected!

> The King of Jyze
> With 40,000 pens
> Marched up to the shed
> And then marched down again.

(But I need better vagueness, better surliness, better
ontological destabilization. I'm letting jyze down, I
know it. In sleep maybe I'll come up with some of that
better stuff. Birthday sleep. Heart of the birthday.
-- Joined by D, I'm hoping. Certainly will go for it.)

[Jyzeburst]

*   *

Far-corner table at the ORB cafe, only real
bookstore. (A flea just materialized in the brambles of
my left forearm; flicked it away.) I mean deep, deep in
the corner. Back among the crumbling bricks, including
even a crumbling brick ceiling. And ancient pipes up
there too, as well as to the immediate rear, one bracing
my chair. And tiny chipped tessellated tiles underfoot.
And on the walls a dozen "Portraits of the Homeless,"
several of whom are well known to me and one who isn't
but looks almost like my double, right down to the ratty
hickory-stripe shirt he's wearing atop a shabby henley.
"Street camo." Maybe I could hire him to play me at
the office on slow nights? -- Not that I'm expecting
many more of those. Or for that matter any other kind.
     And a dish of peach cobbler. A bottle of root
beer. A burst of applause for the author, the one
reading in the next room.
     So this is it, the big actual-day birthday blowout
for Jyzer G, that is, contempo Jyzer G, a/k/a Jyzelby
the Scoper. The true high point of the day (than which
a finer could scarcely be imagined -- by me right now
anyway what with my imagination grounded owing to high-
wind warnings, about which more later -- or then again
maybe not). The home party we've postponed until
Saturday night and the opening of gifts too, of which
there will reportedly be a few, "just little things,"
and rightly so given those same warnings.
     I'm trying to do the twist. The tangle. The
brier-patch whirl. (Scarfing down cobbler lefty,
meanwhile, here and now.)
     -- And am pleased because earlier in the shower I
had some sparky "Jyzer" thoughts. Went on a little
tear, the first in a while. Maybe I'm benefiting from
the job crisis in unexpected ways? Maybe I'll be able
to look at what's still to be done on "Jyzer" -- which
of course is most of it: thirty-five out of a projected
forty first-draft chapters -- with fresh eyes? Maybe my
imagination isn't shut down after all even if grounded?
     No birthday card from sister Barb despite my

80

sending her that hummingbird for hers. Maybe one will straggle in. But I suspect she's made some sort of conscious decision to write off her brothers, or at least this one, much as I decided back in overseas days to write off the entire family. Later I took most of that back, though, and I'm glad I did. (And yet it's sadly true nothing's ever been quite the same again.) Maybe I'll hear more about this from brother Rob -- except Rob may have written me off too, and in a way this would only be right -- me being in high reclusion for so long (high and deep at once!). Then again it would be mostly wrong. We both care. But life conspires against family closeness in this age and particularly in this country. Yet even so I do feel close to them all, and that includes brother Jeff from whom I almost never hear -- he being back in Lahontan, the throbbing heart of the M. zone, the only one left there or anywhere nearby, custodian of Dad's ashes, upholder of all family honor such as it is.

Wallowing in it. Surely no sin on this day.

-- Where will I be for the next one of these? Looks a long way off. Way, way, way out there. Seems farther in a forward direction than the "Viridescence" era is in a backward one, and that's a decade in the rearview now. Ten full flaming years. Wow, he sez. Wow. That's a lot.

Of course I still have millennial hopes. And was there ever a more appropriate time for same? Not for nearly a thousand years anyway, at least in Christian-descent cultures. Likewise I'm determined. I'm focused. I've got it all together or most of it. I know what I like to hear. I fictify pretty good. I nonfictify pretty good. I jyze, I JIFT, I JIRT, I JIFT/JIRT. -- So now juke right outta here. Quick! (Birthday J-burst busted.)

CHAPTER SIX

[Crunch Jyze]

1.

Is this even thinkable? Outdoors in the triangle
at the heart of the historic quarter at dusk? I'll give
it a shot.
Meanwhile the iron jaws are closing. All right,
it's mawkish. It's melodramatic. It's histrionic.
Nonetheless it's true or it feels true. Ugly
triangular steel canines sinking into flesh. Mine.
(Dude tootling a trumpet across the street. It's
the usual scene around here, but early. No live music
yet other than the trumpet. White carriage clop-
clipping by, horse and top-hatted driver and tourists.
Cabs. Drunks. Ancient uneven grayish cobblestones
underfoot. Totem pole rising into the trees. Century-
old brick-and-stone buildings crowding in on all three
sides.)
And it's a holiday. It's Labor Day. I couldn't
let Labor Day slip by without doing a little of the J-
thing, however frantic.
(No one's bugged me so far here on the wooden bench
I've staked out in front of the pizza joint which
itself is lodged boldly between two raucous saloons. A
few dubious gents have sized up the pros and cons and
decided con. Most likely that'll change at some point.)
The news? It won't work with reporter Naomi.
She'd like me to do all her scoping (as I figured she
would) but tax considerations nix the idea (as I feared
they would). Presumably it would be the same story with

reporter Verna -- and Verna didn't even seem all that
troubled when I mentioned to her that if she didn't step
lively the day crew might soon be scoping her stuff.

Meaning what? Meaning I'm thrown back on the mercy
of partner Fran, who's well known to be merciless at
crunch time with those who aren't her good buddies, and
more so with each passing year. And now I'm just about
completely without leverage.

Other bad news: in her birthday call Mother lets it
be known she has emphysema. Not a new diagnosis but one
she'd been keeping hidden. Didn't want to hit her kids
with any more dismaying health info. Now, however, her
tailbone pain is better ("ninety percent better!" were
her words, likely exaggerated) so she's moving ahead
with informing us on the emphysema. What it is not with
Mom is all systems go; it's more like, as she herself
cracked morbid, "all systems gone." At once.

Nonetheless she's a trouper and she's still with
Jim Q. (thank god), she's exercising a lot, she's
getting out for walks (with a cane) (which must be a
sight given her penchant for high drama). She and Jim
are decamping for their winter place next week
(breathing will be easier down there) and in October
they'll try to make it back to the M. zone so they can
meet Angie, brother Jeff's new wife, and "make peace"
with Aunt Shel and Uncle Vern ("thanks to your blazing
the trail last fall I believe I can finally do it").

Now there's jaws, what she's facing. There's
jagged steel incisors. But I still can't feel much
better about my own admittedly relatively extremely
minor situation.

(Two gruff-voiced demands for money so far, one
sales pitch. "You good, man? Got everything you need?"
Yes, next to what these denizens of the triangle here
are up against I've been, and remain, blessed. So that
I and all others of the broadly middle orders will be
induced to think such a thought, of course, guys like
these are denied public support and left to fend for
themselves on the streets. What a pisser of a society
this is. -- The good thing about the seat I'm holding

down being the appearance it fosters that its occupant
is waiting for a bus, the stop itself lying only about
fifteen feet directly in front of the bench. Several
people standing there, others sitting to my right and
left on other benches, most peering forlornly southward
in hopes the reduced holiday schedule will nonetheless
eventually fetch up a holiday clunker coach.)

     -- Streetlights just flicked on. They help, and in
several ways (e.g., make the trees look good).

     Another gorgeous day. Not a cloud. Hard sleeping.
The brain machine whirring and grinding. Again. Hate
to waste all this time. (Drunk staggering, groaning,
muttering about being thrown out of clubs -- he's
barefoot, he stinks. In rags but he'll probably get
mugged anyway: with that shiny new pack of smokes in his
hand he might as well have a big bull's-eye painted on
his noggin.) ("Respectable" types going by too. The
usual mix: local loft-dwellers, young couples in from
outlying districts and burbs, older tourists from cruise
ships, packs of frat boys, navy guys of several nations
on shore leave. Also, at the fairgrounds north of
downtown this is the last day of the big end-of-summer
festival and some revelers from there have drifted down
here.)

     Pleaded Mother, "I know I'm not supposed to ask how
the book's going, but couldn't you just give me a little
hint?" I'm not telling her about the job crisis (other
than there may be one before long), so no, since the two
are linked, I couldn't say much about "Jyzer" either.
I'm grinding out (omitted "fitfully") what may be the
roughest, rawest first draft ever and that's it, what I
told her.

     And that is it. The only point of pride I have at
the moment is my refusal to skip another JIFT/JIRT
"Jyzer" session.

     A fine "surprise" birthday party Saturday when I
got home (about eleven a.m.). And it truly was a
surprise; for some reason I'd been thinking the
celebration was planned for Saturday evening, not
morning. In any event the crowd of "balloon people" who

attended D's and Mama U's birthday parties floated in
yet again, but robustly reinflated, and were joined by
no fewer than eight "Buddhas" (each a big orange-plastic
catfood container shaped like a certain inane cartoon
cat) squatting in a row on the couch and chairs in our
living/dining area ("parlor"), each wearing a hat and
holding a pennant or noisemaker. Funny scene. All
weekend they sat there and the balloon people hovered
above them, making for a two-tiered peanut gallery.
Ice-cream cake, candles, a fine sketch of one of my
scribbler heroes, whose sobriquet (in Japanese) happens
to be "the Scribbler," drawn by the lady herself to hang
with the others in the hallway pantheon (#9 in the
series). Also a bunch of humorous little gifts: "Otter
Crossing" sign, tiny Silver Otter statuette with a
painted toothpick for a lance, used henley (green,
heavy, all three buttons still intact on placket neck),
a catalog picture of a ceramic "Mentoka cow" to be
coming in the mail. And later a second birthday roll in
the hay (an encore!). Very nice. Very good, very fine,
very raunchy birthday. -- Even rented our first video
(from the town store, probably the only place that would
rent to us without a credit card. -- We do have some of
those after all, it turns out, by the way, but only the
replica cardboard type that come unsolicited in the mail
and say "your name here." D snapped out an eighteen-
inch-long wallet cellophane folder of them for laughs at
the store. It seems she's been carrying that wallet
around for weeks awaiting just such an opportunity.)
     (Now a yelling match right behind me: drunk brown
local guys panhandling, drunk pink Aussies arrogantly
telling them to fuck off, drunk brown local guys
following and taunting -- we're all watching warily.
But the brawl's moving out of range. -- And strolling
by, a pristine mixed couple, he a dazed-looking redhead
in a football jersey and she a fresh-faced East Asian
foreign student, I'd wager, who looks and even walks a
little like D and makes me go aww....) (And now the
brawl's back -- ten feet to my rear. Flesh on flesh,
fists, kicks, thuds -- crowd gathering, cries of

encouragement) ---
                        *
     (Had to stand up there for a while. All this
swirling right behind my bench. It's still going on,
the taunting -- and here's a guy pissing into the trash
can right next to me, "Shorty," one of the brawlers --
Latino Afrusan/brown guy like the rest, no shirt, bloody
lip. "You were really rollin' there, bro," some
sycophant says to him. Dude's falling-down wrecked.)
     No cops in sight. -- It's about to break out again
three or four benches down ---
                        *
     -- Well, there go the bellowing Aussies. Nobody
badly hurt. No big deal. (It's always half a surprise
they don't say hey, why fight each other, let's go get
that guy taking notes -- the jyzer.) (Pushing in the
hinged lid of a trash can to piss inside, that's a new
one on me, though I can see it makes a kind of sense and
could even be called civic-minded, considering the
absence of public restrooms around here.)
     Peace returns to the 'rangle. (I didn't mention it
before: a mere century ago the city's last known lynching
-- a triple one -- took place a few steps to my left.
That was about the same time as the worst of the anti-
Chinese riots, also near here. Racial brawls are
nothing new in these precincts. Maybe even a few have
been started by nonhowlers -- nonpinks -- though not any
that I've heard about or witnessed, tonight's included.)
     Strings of twinkling white lights trickle through
the maples overhead. Coupla bar-hoppin' babes in jiggly
halter tops saunter by insouciantly, I guess I could say
on behalf of the rest of the ogling guys.
     ("How you doin', bro?" -- a greeting to make you
tense up these days, fight-or-flee readiness.)
     Elsewise what? Never did hear from a sibling for
my birthday. Had a surprisingly intimate talk with Lan
on the ferry -- learned she came over from Vietnam ten
years ago, her Vietnamese fiance was six-ten (yes!) and
died in his sleep at age thirty from unknown causes (it
happens often with Vietnamese immigrant men of all

sizes, she says, something like an extreme form of
culture shock); and she's now engaged to a six-five
howler who was her instructor in electrical engineering
at the U -- she showed me pix. She's about five-one,
I'd say. I like her and find her sexy-attractive but
she's way too straight for the likes of me -- engineer
straight no less -- and too often I can't follow her
talk. Believe it or not, I'm trying to make sure she
doesn't get too interested in me, possibly as a
forbidden bad boy or, heaven forfend, an exotic
literatus, or even both rolled into one, just in case.
     (Myself, I'll be able to stay detached. Won't I?
I think so. At least I have lots of practice at it. It
hasn't even been hard. But I suppose a hormonal relapse
is always possible. After all I'm still a U.S. male.
And who knows what might happen at home: it's also
always true I could be dumped tomorrow or next week or
next month. Lose my job, lose my home, could easily lose
my woman too. For all these years I've basically viewed
it as an ongoing miracle that it hasn't happened yet.
Except for the one time it did happen, of course, if only
briefly: when the sweet-talking Marco R. rode into town.)
     -- Saloon band warming up. Drummer. Vocalist
testing one-two-three SCREECH. (A drunk now pawing
through the piss-drenched trash can looking for pizza
scraps -- or pissa scraps -- yuck!) ("Hey writer. Can
you help out a brother in need?" -- Bellowing, menacing
voice. Look him hard in the eye and say can't. Dude
might lunge at me, do who knows what. But he moves on.
-- It was one of our local heroes formerly engaged in the
brawl.)
     -- Oh, but I didn't mention something and now
talking about losing my home has reminded me. The firm
is moving too. The investment outfit one floor down has
an option on our space and they're exercising it (they
already have the other end of our floor). Likely date is
November 1. So I'd say that's also likely when I'll be
out of a job, if not before. Partner Fran's letter a
month ago spoke of "at least two months," and we're
extremely busy now so the reprieve might stretch out an

extra month or more, though no one's said anything to me one way or the other. All three dayscopers are taking their remaining vacation for the year in the next six weeks: another sign the game's about over.

My strategy now? Such as it is? Guess I'll go ahead and work up a memo explaining why I think their decision to cut the nightscoping position is risky and propose several options that might work better. But the sad truth is it's doubtful they'll even read it.

(Now a new fight, a man yelling at a woman, next bench. Those nasty Aussies are still around too. They're so offensive that a group of U.S. Navy guys, though mostly Cawk, look ready to come in on the black Latinos' side, which may be unprecedented in all of USAn history -- Civil War possibly excepted. The bugle any second now. It's like a giant trash-talking mosh pit down here. So better shut this down. Now.)

*   *

-- Kwikjyze postscript, safely locked in the office with its "seven levels of security." The inner sanctum, small gray oval table, a big watercolor depiction of a tranquil city beach hanging more than slightly askew on the wall opposite. Or no, it's not even hanging, I see now; it's propped up on a rubber glove and a crumpled cracker box on the counter. So tacky this outfit is becoming in its declining days!

It was a little dicey but I made it up here through the neo-noirish streets without further major incident.

Quiet building tonight.

Why a postscript? No very good reason. Maybe I just wanted to assure myself I'd survived jyzin' in the 'rangle.

Or to mention something I neglected to note back there. D and I talked about where we'll be moving to next. And we tentatively agreed it'll be a bare-bones apartment either in the home port or back in this city right here, preferably in the more racially mixed southern part, whose northern edge lies within a few feet of where I was jyzin' in the 'rangle.

Or maybe because it's Labor Day I simply wanted to

88

honor my place of labor. Why the heck not. Employer,
you were good to me for a number of years. If you
could've found a way not to mess me up with the RIF I'd
like to think you would've. I'd like to think even now
as I jyze you're resolutely mapping out a way to make it
all good again.
        -- Thirty this.

                          2.

        Tired. Fine. Maybe I'll be able to get back into
the kind of free-form jyzing these pages seem to
tolerate best. Though I doubt it. Too much is
happening.
        Not at this minute though. Not hardly. 'Long
about midnight or maybe one a.m. Distant jazz playing.
D's asleep and I'm posted in the "parlor." Ensconced.
In my favorite brown armchair. The birthday peanut
gallery is gathered across from me a few feet away,
hovering above the couch and perched on it and a chair.
Many of the non-Buddhas are now shriveled and deflated
(again), still hanging together but only just barely.
Smiles sagging and jowls dragging. Shifting about
restlessly, even ominously, with each little waft of
draft and especially the jyzer's experimental long-
distance huffs and puffs. Big bad wolf must be pretty
scary over here. In any case the molded-plastic
cartoon-cat-Buddhas are holding steady.
        Does the screw keep twisting? Indeed it does. (Or
metal teeth crunching into bone, however I was putting
it last. Or just say big rumblings from the RIF zone.)
        First I decided to hell with it, I wouldn't write
that long memo to the partners. Better I should
accustom myself to the idea of finding a new job. I was
due for a change anyway. Time to get on with it.
        That very night when I arrived at the office, an
angry letter from Fran. She and Una had discovered that
the dayscoper crew had been slipping out of the office

during slow periods, sometimes for two or three hours at
a stretch, taking turns covering for each other. The
partners were very upset. (This is such crap I can
barely force myself to write it.) What's more they'd
been "startled to realize" I, the nightscoper, had been
working a full forty hours a week during the slow times
instead of my old thirty-hour minimum. This too was
very upsetting to them. Finally, they were "leaning"
toward choosing Amy for the second scoper position --
Fran felt she must inform me of this. The official
decision would be made by the 15th, that is, ten days
from the date of the letter, five days from right now as
I write these words. -- Oh, and they were also
displeased with me because I'd "obviously" been reading
transcripts "too closely" -- they weren't sure whether
this meant they were bad at giving instructions or I was
bad at following them (as if no other possible
explanations existed). And then signed "agonizingly."

     This letter was such a crock I knew all hope was
lost. I whipped off a reply to Fran saying she needn't
"agonize"; if she and the others preferred Amy I would
turn in my scoper's badge with no hard feelings. But I
did want to point out that they'd put me on a forty-
hour week eighteen months ago (I attached a copy of the
memo of understanding about this which Fran herself had
initialed at the time, as had I). And the "reading too
closely" was equally unfounded, and I explained why in
detail (it's not worth going into here). And if I was
currently unable to perform certain complex computer
operations, as Fran's letter also noted, it was because,
as I reminded them, they'd decided not to train me on
those; they'd told me my scoping was "too valuable" to
be spending any of my time on them. -- But whoa, I
didn't want to get carried away. Maybe we could still
work something out on a part-time or per-page basis, I
wrote, and I hoped they would try to keep an open mind,
as I also would try my best to do; and speaking of
crocodile tears, why, did they realize I'd first gone
to work for them fifteen years ago this very month?
     -- Did I say too much is happening? Actually that

pretty much covers it. I left the letter on Fran's desk
Wednesday morning and now it's Sunday and still no
reply. You'd think she'd at least be quick to apologize
to a longtime employee for the false charges she made
based on her own memory lapse. But no such luck. It's
turning out she's become even smaller and meaner than I
thought. This being a fact (and that it is a fact I'll
insist even without presenting sufficient supporting
evidence, though I could certainly do that if necessary)
-- a fact which it does me no good at all to know.

The faster I can put all this behind me the better.

(And the peanut gallery groans again. All through
this it's been groaning. Who knew the voice of fate
could be so consoling?)

-- My letter also said the end of October would be
a good stopping point for me and asked how it would suit
them. No reply on this yet either, but I expect they'll
go along with it, if only because they'll be needing to
have me around for relief work (in effect) while the
dayscopers are using up their vacation time earlier in
the month.

Still to be dealt with is the question of working
directly for individual reporters. Reporter Verna did
express interest in this option this week and said she
and reporter Naomi, who's also interested, would confer
with partner Una about it as soon as Una gets back from
the far coast (I think that's where she is -- the
absence of her moderating influence going a long way to
explain Fran's unusual harshness). It seems, according
to Verna, who informed Naomi of this, the tax problems
can be gotten around. A workable solution might still
emerge. But if so the firm probably won't allow it; it
just makes too much sense personally for Naomi and Verna
to go outside, meaning to me, with their scoping. And
if they do, the other reporters will want a similar
arrangement with an independent scoper and before long
the office will have to shut down its in-house scoping
operation and the poor partners won't have any peons to
order around or to do a major portion of the partners'
own work at the other reporters' expense (the dirty

little secret everybody knows about but no one dares to
mention in this difficult period).

     And unless everyone's real nice to me all of a
sudden, I might not accept whatever solution they thrash
out. I'm again thinking a change of jobs could be
preferable. I'm even a little excited about the notion
(at times). D and I are both reading the want ads.
Tomorrow she'll be checking out some sort of pottery-
throwing piecework gig (at ten cents a pot I don't think
it's the answer -- but it might be a start on one). I'm
again hauling home empty boxes for moving purposes.
We'll eventually need to be renting long-term storage
space, most likely. And I'm dreaming about six months
of unemployment pay during which I could devote all my
energies to "Jyzer" and maybe even get moving on
"Mentoka Dreams." Six months in the fictojyzone -- it
just might be enough.

     Meanwhile I'll continue to go in on Sundays to
print the proofed protojyze and type up the last volume
of the spree. If things work out as I'm hoping I'll
have seven weeks or so to finish up these projects and
that should be just about right. I might even let the
firm provide the toner and paper for them as a form of
severance pay since I'm about to run out of both. Tacky
of the partners not to offer a single penny of severance
after my decade and a half of stellar service. So maybe
I'll be equally tacky. Maybe I'll take them at their
literal word on the sanctioned printing of my own stuff
just as I did on "your scoping is too valuable."

     I'd like to regain some focus on "Jyzer" but I know
it's beyond me right now. I mutter to myself about
tough-mindedness but I'm still consumed for most of my
waking hours (including those when I should be sleeping
but can't) by obsessive thoughts about the job crisis.
It just burns me up -- but I'm sure as hell not about to
let anyone at the office know that. Wouldn't want to
give them the satisfaction. (No, I don't take well to
being RIF'd. No, I don't like being unappreciated.
That's just how it is. So what. -- Shut up, balloons.
You too, Buddhas.) (If you meet a Buddha on the couch,

diss him. Eight Buddhas, same. Eight Buddhas in
orange-plastic cartoon-cat disguise, wearing ratty hats
originally worn by the jyzer himself, diss to the max.)
    What's worst about all this? It may turn out to be
my next job, whatever it is. But right now it's the
idea of moving again. Not idea; necessity. The house
may already be sold -- to D's friend Marissa (my least
favorite among her friends, not that it matters). Sale
to Marissa would actually be a blessing because we could
take our time in moving. For the most part Marissa and
her husband, Curtis (a quiet fellow of Chinese descent,
incidentally, whereas she's a highly noisy howler),
would be mostly absentee landowners, just like the U's
themselves. Still we could never afford to pay the rent
they'd charge on the place -- even with a friendship
discount, which no one has proposed or offered just yet
as far as I know -- and we'd have to bail, probably by
the end of next summer. Or if the Marissa/Curtis deal
falls through, the U's would put the house on the market
in May or June. In that case D and I would have eight
or nine months to get our act together, starting now. I
shudder to think of the labor involved.
    So I won't think about it. Instead I'll focus on
all the masterpieces I'm not blazing out. Oops --
there goes another one up the flue. Holy smoke, so to
speak, and my time left on Earth's ever shrinking. Drat
the luck, boo hoo, boo hoo, groan groan groan.
    -- And that'll be it for this round. Got to start
girding up for Thursday and the news on partner Fran's
decision -- actually just four days from now by
Gregorian time as opposed to NUT -- which, in case I
haven't explained it before, is Nightscoper Upside-down
Time, under which the day starts at four p.m. and so
always trails the Gregorian day by two-thirds of a
circadian cycle or, in other words, sixteen hours.
    A lucky find, this literary form called jyze.
Keeps me distracted. Catharted. Sane if I'm too crazy
and crazy if I'm too sane. Even lets me feel minimally
productive when nothing else is working out.
    -- So how's that as a positive thought for today's

[Jyzeburst]

benediction, O peanut gallery?
    "Right on, Jyzer G! Your jyze is a crock but you
totally rock!"

                            3.

        Crunch time. Right now. I mean the true crunch.
The white envelope awaits me. The fate of nightscoper G
will reveal itself at last.
        It's right up there. Two blocks to the south,
other side of the street, the top dozen floors visible
from here and the rest hidden behind other, lesser,
buildings. Floodlit off-white with white-blinded
windows. Towering above it the top two-fifths or so of
the truly massive structure that stands a block
diagonally farther down, the lights of its crowning
pyramid also freshly ablaze. "The Great White Wall of
Commerce." And here I sit, yes, Jyzelby of Jyze City.
        I know the white envelope's up there because I saw
it last night. It's snowy white except where it bears
my name (first and last, bold computer headline font)
and the firm's logo (the two initials of the partners'
last names riding atop the city skyline with the
celebrated golf-tee icon poking up between them to serve
as a quirky ampersand), and it's sealed. Rather than
open it last night and possibly tip someone off to my
extracurricular presence in the office, I thought I'd
stretch out the suspense a bit longer. Prepare myself
mentally.
        So here I am. Midtown plaza park at deepest dusk,
a few paces from the roaring "curtain of water" fountain.
I'm perched atop the bandstand, far eastern side, my
back resting against one of the marble arch supports (or
less an arch than a huge heavy-duty pastel staple) and
my feet planted on one of the bandstand steps. This
park is also triangular in shape, like the one I was
visiting last week, and from where I sit the long sides

of the triangle here seem to make a spearhead pointing
directly at -- the white envelope.

 A late-season warm spell. It's not even chilly at
the moment, though the breeze is picking up and it soon
will be. Park nearly empty. Lollipop trees and
unliable-on, sectioned-off benches. Big franchise
bookstore still open across the street (which runs one-
way from the direction I'm facing, so it's streaming
lots of jiggly incandescent lights right at me). A
few skateboarders, a couple of bicycle cops. Pastel
paving stones everywhere. Not a bad place -- the big
civic accomplishment of a decade ago. (A guy is now
hunkered down directly opposite me with his back
resting against the other staple leg, stage right plus
a foot as opposed to my stage left plus a foot --
twentyish cawk in a black baseball cap worn backwards,
he's gnawing on a sub sandwich and peering morosely at
the beat-up purple skateboard squeezed phallically
upright between his thighs -- and that's a fact.)

 What a week. Terrific stuff -- all the elements.
High drama. Grinding work. Disease. Hilarity and
madness. Hot sex. (For some reason, probably related
to all the above but who knows, D and I are suddenly
screwing like minks.)

 Do I even want to try to spell it all out?
"Construct a narrative"? Hell no! This is jyze!

 But in short, Monday I left reporter Naomi a note:
if she were ever to make a move, it said, now would be
the time. Wednesday night she left me a note: she and
reporter Verna had spoken with partner Una at lunch and
Una had agreed the firm would let me stay on to do
grand jury. Naomi pressed for more: she'd like to have
me doing all her stuff. Una said no, they needed to
keep the dayscoping crew busy. (Oh yeah? So why
don't the partners have them working on their own stuff
then, except off the books? Huh? Huh? For shame!)

 Would grand jury alone, Naomi wondered in her note,
be enough to keep me coming in? Probably not, I wrote
back, but maybe: all would depend on what terms the
partners would accept. And Fran had said they would let

me know their decision by the 15th, which was the next
day.

No doubt Fran hit the roof over Una's concession on
grand jury. This would mess up her nice neat (albeit
bloody) meat-ax approach. It would make her look bad:
she'd already told me no guaranteed hours, and grand
jury would in essence be guaranteed because it meets two
days every week with few exceptions. From evidence
spotted around the office I know Fran was scrambling at
the last moment to change the contents of that white
envelope.

Oddly enough, or maybe not so oddly -- who the hell
knows from oddly anymore with such bizarre doings? --
I'd had one of those eureka moments right before getting
Naomi's note about Una's concession. On the way in that
very night I'd decided to hell with it, I was moving on.
Unemployment for me. The big gamble. "Better to rule
in hell than serve in heaven."

(Here's some guy with a long stick trying to
dislodge a golden cord from the crossbeam of the staple
about ten feet up. A golden cord? Yes. What's that
doing up there? Is it a fleece disguised as a cord?
Could the (mythical?) argonaut guy be about to
materialize right here in our famously argonautical
town? But never mind, drop it.)

So I was on a high. Yes we would go for it. The
new life. "You must change your" -- so why not me? I'd
wrung all I could out of the firm anyway. Not for me
one more moment of this absurd turmoil. -- And
therefore the news of Una's concession didn't thrill me
when I first learned about it from Naomi's note. Grand
jury, big deal. The very best I could do from that
would be seven or eight hundred bucks a month, roughly
the equivalent of a full-time minimum-wage job, and
probably the firm would offer less or even much less
(nobody had spoken of pay rates).

Over the next couple of days I reversed myself on
this. The key realizations: at most I'd have to work
only two six-hour nights and one three-hour night a
week, leaving most of the normal five-day workweek free

for fictojyzing; and I'd be eligible for partial
unemployment (because my weekly hours would shrink from
forty to fifteen or fewer). The firm's pay plus the
partial unemployment would be enough to allow D and me
to squeak by for a six-month period even if she should
fail to find a job or be unable to hold one for health
reasons. And: I'd continue to have the full
unemployment option in reserve should I get RIF'd again,
say from fifteen hours to zero.

        (They're still working on the golden cord. What's
up, fellas? A Middle Eastern language. Maybe some sort
of religious festival was held here. Or maybe a
clandestine lynching, who knows. For sure these guys
with the sticks -- three guys now, three sticks, just as
with those argonauts of antiquity if memory serves (this
is not a setup; this is sheer coincidental real time) --
for sure these guys don't look like religious types or
mythical types either. They remind me of a trio of
backwoods dudes (probably militia, so of course Cawks) I
once witnessed ripping off copper wire from telephone
poles within a mile of U Acres. -- And they bring to
mind as well the deer who were standing on their hind
legs in the yard this morning while stretching full
length to nibble at mid-tree apples. One stag and two
mamas, along with two fawns grazing below. Made it easy
to see how giraffes might've evolved. -- As now a tour
group wanders by and shouts encouragement to the stick
guys.)

        The 15th, Thursday, came and went with no word on
the final decision and also no word on why the delay.
-- All along it's been almost as if we're two foreign
countries dealing through intermediaries. Since this
crisis began I've seen none of the principals in the
flesh for a single second, excepting a brief talk with
Verna one night as she rushed to pick up her kids (and
she's the most peripheral player for sure). And also
the one even briefer morning exchange with Naomi
mentioned earlier, which I'd almost forgotten about.

        By Friday I had come back around to pretty much the
same position I'd settled on a week earlier. Realizing

I was likely destined to fail, I would nonetheless keep
trying to squeeze the firm for a decently paid part-time
job. The difference was that now for the first time I
had some real leverage: Una's promise to Naomi. The
unchanged aspect was that there had been no concession
on pay rates. If they wanted to get rid of me they
still could: offer the job but chop the pay. Obvious.
And there was nothing I could do about it. Except
argue. Or go to Naomi and say in effect, "I told you
I'd stay but now I can't because they're trying to cut
my pay to the bone, please do something." Probably
wouldn't work but, again, a slim chance it would.

  And that's where things still stand. I've tried to
imagine what Fran's letter will say and of course I've
been obsessing on possible responses. One way or
another she'll doubtless hurl some outrageous charges at
me. The main thing is not to fly off the handle in
responding. Play my cards as if I'm leading from
strength. Make it clear I'm ready to tell the firm to
take this job and shove it, but don't be so crude or
foolish as to come right out and say it.

  (The golden cord's still hanging untouched up
there. The sticks didn't work; the argonaut gang have
vamoosed. And to the south, yes, the white wall is
still looming too, as is the firm's row of windows,
which I might note is now wastefully lit up like all the
rest. Why? For the janitors, of course, though they
won't be coming around for several more hours. And for
me, I suppose, in a few moments. But when you get right
down to it, for the sheer power-flexing arrogance of the
display. The whole downtown's doing it. In many cases
it goes on all night long. Idiocy! But also: "Just how
it is.")

  As for the promised tale of pestilence, I got hit
with a bad cold in the middle of all this. No doubt
stress and lack of sleep "lowered my resistance." And
of course this would also turn out to be the toughest
grand-jury week of the entire year: whereas the ordinary
week has two full days of testimony, and sometimes only
one, this week had five. So I've been scrambling like

crazy. This is not the time to start giving Naomi and Verna sloppy, hastily scoped transcripts. My strategy has been to take a couple of sick days but to show up for work anyway (the day crew has no way of knowing whether I've done this unless they come in late at night or call and check while I'm there, and of course if I'm there I know whether they've come in or called and can adjust my claims accordingly).

What else this week? Nothing. Except the Eurusan explorer's travel journal finally arrived, but I've scarcely had a chance to look at it. And the major league baseball season has been canceled outright. Oh yes: and U.S. invasion of a small Caribbean nation appears imminent. Just another outrageous criminal act under international law, no big deal. Nothing even slightly unusual.

So, am I ready? Got to get a bite to eat. Don't want to show up at the office too early, but it's cold out here now: I'm risking pneumonia to scratch out this deathless jyze. And also risking a knife in the side (not the back; four feet of marble's got that) (but the front's wide open too) (and for that matter the golden cord could drop around my neck at any moment and tighten, then hoist -- to which I'd simply say: up yours, Jason!).

And after the bite, head on over to the office. Rip open Fran's letter and read. And ponder. Maybe come back to these pages later. Or maybe not.

But in any case: the white envelope, please.

*   *

And the winner is -- me! The nightscoper! The jyzer, the contempo one right here! Jyzelby! Yes!

Am I reading this correctly? Am I dancing in place and clicking my heels in the air? Am I wielding the big stick and twirling the golden cord? OR WHAT?

"Ask not for whom the market economy RIFs, O Jyzelby; it RIFs for thee!"

Restraint. Hold on. Nothing's signed yet. Lots could still go wrong. And even if it doesn't, this is not the lottery. Not talking about millions of bucks

here, yachts and endless free time, a new brand-X pen
with custom-ground ultra-oblique nib. Just talking
about a lousy part-time nighttime day-job, and not an
easy one either -- and one with a superlong commute.
     However. It looks good. It looks very good. On
salary I might be coming out twenty-five percent better
than my best-case hope while still retaining the free
time for fictojyzing, the free four and a half days
with only two and a half days a week (more like a long
weekend) required for work. So -- WHOOEE!
     Say it is so, Joe! (Jason? Herman? Arthur?)
     This at the big conference table. Here's where I
came to brace myself before tearing open the envelope
and reading the letter.
     Yes, the expected outrages are there. (Partner
Fran "can't remember" okaying my move from thirty to
forty guaranteed hours a week and therefore it didn't
happen, even though I've given her a photocopy of the
memo on this matter which she initialed -- and this
mulishness coming from a certified notary public, mind
you!) -- But no matter. I'm willing to forget it like
all the other outrages amassed over the years. Let's
keep our priorities straight here. Like the man said,
far, far, far better to serve in heaven than rule in
hell. (Do I contradict myself? Very well, I do that.
-- And this heaven has its other compensations.)
     The big breakthrough, and a surprise it is:
suddenly Fran's agreeable to paying me on a page-rate
basis as an independent contractor. This is something I
began advocating a decade ago and have brought up to the
partners intermittently ever since, including in my
letter to Fran last month which she so brusquely
dismissed. Better yet, the rate she's proposing is,
almost unbelievably, far higher than the one I was
planning to suggest. I was set to enter an opening bid
of sixty cents a page, but I would've settled for fifty-
five, maybe even fifty. She's offering eighty! And
that's after deducting a dime a page for use of their
machines!
     It seems I didn't know my own market value. She

includes a printout of internet info showing market
rates for scopers as high as a dollar a page, then
devotes two long paragraphs to explaining why the firm
can offer me only eighty!

The main thing now is I don't want to appear too
eager to accept.

No official confirmation in her letter that October
31st will be my last day as an employee but no denial
either so I'm assuming that's the deal. Fine with me.
This gives me six weeks to fit myself out as an
independent contractor. And to tend to various other
transitional acts as well, including most likely a good
number I'm not aware of yet.

-- At eighty cents a page I figure I can clear
twenty bucks an hour no problem -- maybe even thirty.
To clear twenty I need to scope at a rate of about
thirty pages an hour (considering the time needed for
punching in corrections and other peripheral tasks).
I'm used to scoping at forty pages an hour and up. Our
standard speed for the firm is supposed to be sixty-five
pages an hour! (Not that anyone could ever do that on a
sustained basis without churning out lots of garbage.)

I'm just stunned. Chin-on-the-floor stunned.
Shocked jyzeless, almost. Technically I'm still being
RIF'd -- fired -- but in actuality I'm about to be
granted a hefty raise. And yet dayscopers Doris and Amy
are being kept on at the same rates they were being paid
before. The winners lose and the loser wins!

How is this possible? Damned if I know. But
evidently it's because the firm's pay scale for scopers
has fallen far behind the market. None of us have had a
raise in five years. We didn't know what was going on
out there in the real world, not to mention the virtual
world. Maybe online scopers can charge more because
they're working at home and using their own (highly
expensive) equipment and thus can pass on to their
clients lots of overhead for rent and depreciation; and
they're setting the rates for all scopers since they're
the only ones in demand. So: no wonder Cathy moved on
and Thomas is about to.

How will Doris and Amy react when they hear? It'll
be a kick to see. Maybe I should move fast on nailing
down the eighty cents before they find out and start
screaming. As they'd have good reason to do. The firm
couldn't afford to pay all of us at that rate, I'm quite
sure. But then again a bigger portion of what Doris
and Amy do (one third as opposed to my one sixth or so)
is not scoping; it's performing routine computer
operations. Supposedly that's part of why my pay rate
has been higher than theirs all along, together with
more years of service and the "combat bonus" for working
nights.
     -- To heck with all that. Worry later. Savor now.
Can it be? I'm in? Over the hump? Like...magic?
Like...what's the catch? Like...who's fooling whom?
What's going on? Has my ship come in? My gravy train?
When do we roll? Gangway, lemme on!
     Got to, just got to be a catch. Either that or
they've realized I'm the catch but in another sense --
and how could that so suddenly be?

CHAPTER SEVEN

[Jyze Bulletins from the RIF'd Zone]

1.

     Still lost in post-nap groggy mind. Here in the
new chalky-white attic room perched on a chair I quietly
hauled up just moments ago. By the window, looking out
at "the crack of dawn," or so I intended -- the aubadian
moment! -- but it's a little later than that now.
     Silvery sunrise. Sun just starting to edge over
evergreen-serrated ridgeline. Green football-field-

length incline of meadowy lawn reaching way up to the
barn at the far end is shimmering silverishly itself,
the usual heavy dew looking in this light more like
frost. Saggy cedar barn slouching almost black -- it's
no barn really, just a very large shed with a high
barnlike roof. Wall of green forest pressing close in a
semicircle behind it. My own much smaller cedar shed,
only beginning to age patchily gray and black sort of
pinto-like, standing partly out of sight behind a woodsy
green promontory halfway up the incline to the left.
First time I've seen all this from such a high angle
(even if from the low end of the hill).

But here comes the rest of the sun. I'm staring
right into it -- have to move my chair a foot to the
left. This way a plywood sheet blocking half the new
window (they had to punch a hole through the gable to
put it in) also blocks the sun.

It's a fine new garret room up here, ceiling
truncated, if that's the word, on both sides, tilted or
angled downward except for a foot-wide flat strip
running just beneath the peak beam of the house. The
walls are freshly sheetrocked, with streaks of joint
compound still showing. The floor is bare plywood and
littered with construction debris: sawdust, nails,
stripping paper, scraps of metal flashing, a stub of
wide yellow carpenter pencil. Fragrant fresh wood smell
mingling with dank old attic smell. And here's a big
tub of the joint compound, looks like maybe ten gallons
-- sixty-one pounds, it says.

Birds going at it out there though not sending up
the usual sunrise wall of sound. Could be it's already
too late in the year for that. Any turning leaves in
sight? No. But I know for a fact plenty exist in other
realms just barely out of view. (A couple of unusually
tall spindly-legged sawhorses nuzzling each other like
colts at the far south end of the carport roof, which is
flat and fenced almost like a small corral, just outside
the window here. Wish I could toss them some carrots.)

D sleeps. But I'd better mention right now the
newest hit of bad news. Her yearly physical last week

detected a polyp growing either on one of her ovaries or
on her uterus, she's not sure which, but "somewhere up
there." Thursday she goes in for a biopsy. Chances of
malignancy are less than one in twenty, which beats
Russian roulette but by nowhere near enough to lower our
anxiety levels. (I'm being real quiet so she won't hear
me up here. She's likely to want to come up and ply me
with cautions. This will be her room, her safe
sanctuary when she's alone in the house, once we figure
out how to mount a heavy-duty lock and bolt on the
inside of the door, which is exactly as wide as the steep
stairwell leading up from it. She's already let her
parents know they'll have to drag her out of the house
now that she has, or almost has, this room. It's part of
our strategy for wangling another year or two of
subsidized residency at U Acres. I've persuaded her it's
in her own best interest: if we can hang on here she
might not have to go to work. If we have to move out and
pay rent, we'll definitely need some income from her.)
     Corey the carpenter and one of his crew (during my
week of wearing earplugs and sleeping in the basement --
farthest corner of the house -- as they hammered and
power-sawed up here) -- both of them commented to me
separately and also to D about what a perfect writer's
studio this garret room would make. And they're right.
Too perfect? No. Just ideal. But I'm already well
set. D claimed this room from the start. It just took
five years and the prospect of having to sell the house
to convert it to highest and best use.
     -- Also she was deathly sick for two days last week.
Vomiting godawful yellow stuff, bilelike. I'm wondering
if it could be morning sickness. The pattern seems wrong
for that but it's still possible. Too bad we don't know
right now: if tests proved positive maybe the doctors
could deal with the matter while removing the polyp.
(Fetus lovers we're not. And regardless of that, several
doctors have warned she'd be seriously risking her life
to give birth.)
     -- And the RIF crisis? This turned out to be
hiatus week. I wrote partner Fran a five-page letter

accepting her offer of part-time page-rate scoping at eighty cents a page. She read the letter the next day and it's been riding a stack of papers on her desk ever since. No reply. No confirmation, no haggling over terms, no withdrawal of the offer. So far. Could be her mind's on other things (bigger fish) since she's scheduled to give a speech at an industry convention somewhere out of state this week. Probably the speech will expound on ways to cut back scoping staff so as to finance a more elaborate computer system. (No joke; she lies awake at night scheming up new ways to do this -- dayscoper Doris, who continues to be one of her best buds, told me so.)

At this point it hasn't even been confirmed I'll have my full-time job through October. Fran can't be bothered. Yet Doris's vacation begins today and she'll be gone two full weeks and we're the busiest we've been all year -- so much so that even with all four remaining scopers, myself included, working overtime last week we weren't able to keep up. It'll be amusing to see what happens if the rush continues. Poor Fran's timing was not good. Almost from the day she announced the RIF we've been wildly busy. (Dayscoper Thomas will be moving back east, Doris told me, after his last day on November 30. But he'd already given notice months ago.)

Last Monday evening I ran into reporter Naomi on the sidewalk outside our building lobby (she was pulling her little reporter cart) and I informed her about Fran's page-rate offer and said I was planning to accept it. She literally jumped for joy. Then I told her Fran had said she'd charge her and reporter Verna ninety cents a page to be able to pay me eighty. "What's the other dime for?" Naomi indignantly wanted to know. After all it costs the firm next to nothing to have me working on their machines at night -- we figure an incremental penny or two per page tops.

Later I called Verna and we talked about the same thing -- Fran's motives. Why would she make me this offer which would raise Naomi's and Verna's rates without asking them first? Was this a clumsy attempt

to sour them on hiring me? (If so, why present the
offer to me first? Why not go to them first with the
info regarding the rate increase and see if they would
veto the idea of offering it to me?) Verna and I
agreed Fran's probably just addled -- lacking in
business sense, especially the people side of things.
"Fran needs to get a life," Verna told me. "Everybody
says so. She's way too involved with computers."

With both Naomi and Verna I left it that they would
look into the matter with Fran at a propitious time.
Apparently none arose this week. Meanwhile I did the
best I could in my letter to Fran (written immediately
after talking with Verna) to undo the possible damage
caused by the ninety-cent charge to Naomi and Verna. I
volunteered to work for only seventy-five cents a page
on non-grand-jury stuff (GJ pages have smaller margins
and on average they're tougher to scope) and I pointed
out the low incremental cost of my using the machines at
night when they'd otherwise be sitting idle.

Also I had to respond to Fran's remarks about the
possibility of my doing fill-in work for the firm on an
hourly basis. That would be fine too, I said, but I'd
need to raise my rates to compensate for their taking
away my benefits. Those are worth about three bucks an
hour to me, I pointed out, so I'd just tack that amount
onto my new hourly rate. Also I'd be adding surcharges
for low guaranteed hours and late notice. -- And it was
probably a mistake to specify that three bucks. It
might shock her. "Seventeen-fifty an hour -- to hell
with him!" But I couldn't resist. After the series of
letters from her with all the outrageous charges and
mulish denials I want to stick it to her real bad. I
also want her to see I was right in warning she'd be
shooting herself and the firm in the foot if she cut out
the nightscoping. No doubt I should've eased up because
she was already eating crow from having to make me the
per-page offer. But no, I wanted to give the knife a
good twist. I still do. Hopefully I won't have to pay
too much for it. I think I've still got her cornered.
She may even be forced to ask me to stay on full-

time. If we continue this busy it's hard to see her
having any other option. If she does ask me to stay,
though, I intend to demand a raise -- from $14.50 to $16
an hour (before benefits, which would continue as now)
and from three weeks' annual vacation to four (to match
Doris, whose years of service trail mine by two). Do I
have the guts to do this? Am I crazy enough? Vengeful
enough? Petty enough? I sure hope so -- all of those.

        -- So that's this week's tale. Not much to it
really but I guess the narrative line (hack hack) has
advanced a little. For my part a lot of the job-related
tension has eased, though probably only temporarily.
Even with all the carpenter noise I could actually sleep
this week (on the office carpet too). Here I am at home
and it's Monday morning -- for the first time in six
weeks I didn't go in to the office on Sunday night.
I've even started thinking "Jyzer" thoughts again.
        Meanwhile it's roughly an hour and a half later
than it was at the start. The sun's moved up high
enough that the apple trees earlier sheltered by the
barn are casting their own impressive downhill shadows.
Dew evaporation lends all this a wavy mirage effect
(probably the roof of the house is steaming as the barn
roof was earlier; if so, from the road it would appear
to be on fire) (the first time Papa U witnessed this
phenomenon he thought the house really was on fire and D
and Mama U tease him about it to this day). -- And my
stomach's been growling the entire period I've been up
here. "Have you noticed?" (Catchphrase of a poem I
came across last night.) -- Yes, I've noticed!
Nowadays the growling always starts up at six-thirty
a.m. sharp, which is the usual time on workdays for
cracking open my dinner box on the homewardbound ferry.
        -- Or notice this: a little pile of joint compound
on the windowsill. Gray. Looks just like ol' Mom's
used chewing gum did when she saved it overnight on the
kitchen counter when I was a kid. And right now the
jyzer's so hungry he could almost try gnawing on it.
        Stop. Halt. Seek real grub.

[Jyzeburst]

2.

     Am I cantankerous tonight? Or do I just not feel
like jyzing? Or am I foolishly embarrassed to have so
little to say? -- It seems! And I'm talking about all
the above.
     Awkward jyzing posture on the couch. In my study.
Feet drawn up. Lamp burning directly above my scalp,
fold-out brass, three intensities and it's on the middle
one and it's heating my hair almost to flashpoint. As I
stare the old black ceramic hippo coin bank in the
nostrils. And right above that a memorabilia shelf.
Dad's tiny sailing trophy I see. The wooden pull car I
gave Elgie as a kid and Lady S later irately gave back.
The observation coach from the electric train Dad gave
me as a kid and his father gave him as a kid. Loads of
stuff gathering dust. (Okay, not "loads." A few meager
pounds and it's about all of what remains from that whole
era, other than a couple of photo albums and a shelf of
protojyze and another shelf of personal papers. Remains
here, that is, in this house and in my shed. Mother and
the sibs would have quite a few more pounds.)
     -- Out from D the doc with gloved' hand hauled a
bloody mass of tissue. Whether malignant or benign we
won't know for two weeks. She drove herself home the
same afternoon and remains cheerful. I'm the one who
cracks anxiety-ridden morbid jokes. (Here's "the hottest
new group in jazz" circa my college years, come to visit
these pages again. A twofer. "Unhand that bottle!"
-- Or maybe it's just a onefer. I guess so. I was
hoping their splendid version of "Jyzeburst" would
modulate on in. But anything these three do is okay by
me. -- Or "Cloudburst" actually, okay.)
     Wall of books. Chest-high stacks of Mentoka
newspapers. Hat rack standing in the far corner with all
pegs occupied (I never wear hats anymore, other than the
"DREAM" lid occasionally for verisimilitude when

fictojyzing). Three-drawer "oak" filing cabinet, desk
made of a standard-size "oak" door propped atop two two-
drawer "oak" filing cabinets. (Are these "oak" items
really oak? A thin veneer maybe.) A blue dragonfly
kite hung on the wall in honor of "The Blue Dragonfly,"
one of the fictive protojyze manuscripts I reprinted
last month. Dark brown wood paneling. Books stacked
and piled everywhere. A row of hummingbird whirligigs.
Calendars. Brother Rob's and D's and Mama U's and my
own framed artwork. A big mola of a robotic red-eyed
face D has labeled "Nightscoper Gets Home, 8:30 A.M.")
     And the job crisis? No RIF riffs?
     It's shaking down now. Another long letter from
partner Fran, basically of little interest. Mainly it
says she's put the page-rate proposal to reporters Naomi
and Verna and is now dropping out of the loop; I can
work things out with them. Obviously she's not too
pleased at being outmaneuvered, she being the Master in
this and all other known Chanceries and wanting me out
of there (if the truth be known) and here I am staying
on under terms she refers to in this letter as "highway
robbery." Yet she proposed them herself! Go figure!
     Next I talked with Naomi. Knowing she wouldn't
want to pay the ninety cents Fran had offered on her
behalf for grand jury, I asked what would work for her.
She said eighty-five was doable but she sounded iffy so
I suggested we go to eighty and she accepted with
relief. Then I went even further: said I would do her
non-grand-jury stuff for seventy, meaning she'd actually
save money by having me rather than the dayscoping crew
do it. Terrific, she said. Of course at the start, by
partner Una's order, only grand jury and other
government work is to be subbed out to me, but Naomi
figures the reduced day crew will soon be overloaded and
she'll be allowed to give me other work. I expect she's
right. (But I'm not too sure I want her to be. I'd
like to keep my workload as light as possible -- but I
also need enough bucks for D and me to live on.)
     Reporter Verna I haven't been able to talk with
yet. Naomi thinks Verna will be delighted with the

eighty-cent grand-jury rate.

My official last day as an employee will indeed be October 31st, four weeks from tomorrow, except I also have a week of vacation coming and thus I won't have to work beyond the 24th, or at least not under the old dispensation. So instead that last week I'll start in on the new dispensation. Not a moment's rest! In the meantime I have to come up with a business license and check into the possibility of partial unemployment pay.

D's idea for naming my independent incorporated scoper self: "Jyzer Ink." (She beat me to it! My own initial idea had been lame indeed: RogueScoper.)

With any luck at all I'll soon be considerably better off than before this whole RIF donnybrook began. Not materially but in ways that matter more. Three, four, even five days off a week, yet I'll still have access to the firm's computers and printers.

Right now I'm not wildly happy. This is stupid, just fear of the unknown, future shock or something. Also we may still have to move out of this house next spring. Also I'm worried about D's health and Mother's and my own (Achilles and low back again). I'm just not in the right frame of mind for celebration. And I'm worried about "Jyzer" -- I want the story to jump out at me as before. So far it's refusing to do that.

("It don't mean a thing if it ain't got that swing" -- utterly apropos musical soundtrack for that paragraph, again provided by the jazz station.)

(Instantly upon setting down the pen -- same No. 5 as always now -- I'll be conking out on this very spot. Snap off the radio first, though, and also the swing-arm lamp, and the wall lamp, but leave the desk lamp on to make waking up easier. Also fetch the red windup alarm clock so I won't sleep through the rest of the night, as I probably would without it, though there'll be no need to set the alarm; from much experience I know just having the clock present and ticking away will be enough. And maybe I won't need a blanket since the blood brought to a boil by the scalp lamp now seems to be heating me down to my nethermost appendages.)

Reach deep. Grope for a few more lines. Maybe mention the merry time D and I had flipping through our old photo albums earlier today. Laughing out loud with each new page. That's us? Check out the shoes! Ho ho, sure outdid ourselves on that one! -- First time in several years for those albums. Strange the way a brush with the Reaper will affect you. -- Or not so strange really. In fact groaningly predictable. But no less affecting for that, at least to me. And to her too, I do believe (and what's more I prefer to!).

3.

Autumn coming on. Red blaze in a tree here and there. Chill in the armpits if I don't wear a henley. Soon a sweatshirt. And the sun's just about completely down by the time the six-twenty pulls in over here, and the morning six-forty going the other way leaves in complete darkness (or close to it) yet the sun's rising by the time the boat docks on the far side.
    Meanwhile a glitch. How bad I don't know yet, but my whole scheme may unravel.
    (First of the continentals is right on time tonight, a terminal worker assures a kid who asks. Echoing voices. Half a dozen of us scattered in the huge waiting room, up from three when I arrived. -- But outdoors the place is spruced up a bit, three-ball light clusters all working now even though the parking lot is nearly empty. And up above, all four faces of the clock tower (a Venetian knockoff, I've now determined) -- all four are lit up, albeit each with a crazily different time, and all four wrong -- I walked around to check.)
    Reporter Verna is the glitch. It appears she's not buying the eighty/seventy plan reporter Naomi was sure she'd jump at. Is she just trying to bargain me down further? Can't say yet. But she's making noises about scoping her own stuff. "Sole support for my family."

She bounces between this and "I've got a life, better to pay a scoper and free up the time." (She's rumored to be dating again.)

Last I spoke with her about this was Monday. It's now Sunday. She was supposed to talk it over with Naomi (who would explain how she can financially justify paying eighty a page) and get back to me, but things always tend to slide with Verna. She's somewhat mysterious, a temperamental artist of a reporter and by far the best steno-writer in the firm.

This week will tell the story. (Each week seems to have a story it will tell, at least lately, and as a jyzer I must be pleased this is so, and am, even though in theory jyze tries to avoid dependence on story.)

(Train whistle whoos off in the distance. "Hm, comin' in early, sounds like." Or more likely it's a freight pulling out of the container yards. Now the approaching rumble. Optimists and epigones heading out the door pushing baggage carts. -- Yup, a freight. Now the sheepish returns, along with a bracingly cold and ozone-scented and autumn-leaves-blowing draft.)

What will I do if Verna says no to eighty? Guess I'll dangle seventy-five. Maybe even seventy. Hate to do it but I'll soon be desperate, let's face it. We're down to three weeks until my last day.

And if Verna's set on self-scoping no matter what? I'll still have Naomi's grand-jury/government work, but that will pay only four to five hundred a month on average, and that's before expenses, taxes, etc. About unemployment pay I still know nothing. Should be able to squeeze a few bucks out of them, but at what cost in hassle? Won't know for a while. No unemployment office anywhere along my daily route -- have to go way up north in the city (near our first rental house) or to the vicinity of our car dealer on the other side (a forty-mile round trip, not doable unless I take a day off).

-- Now the real arrival. Soon the swarm. Silver cars backing by just outside, ding ding ding.

If Verna relents we'll be all right. But I'm worried.

(And here they are already and as usual they're
surprising in all their particularity, I guess I could
say: this person and this one and this one each for a
different reason pops up here looking like this and this
and this, and in each and every case you wonder why --
very quick wondering usually -- and what it all means to
them, being here, this dilapidated depot, this remote
city with all its own particularity, including this odd
quasi-grungy fellow here pushing a J-stick.)
     Worried about what else? The bloody tissue mass --
what was it? This week we'll know. (To forestall
repeated calling, the co-op now sets a "phone
appointment" for revealing biopsy results; ours is
Thursday.) Little talk about it though. The odds are
good but the fright level is still high. In its iron
grip try to be stoic and laugh a lot -- but not too
much.
     (All this going down with travelers crowding
around, thighs and hips and buns jostling up close right
at my eye and nose level -- here and there a reeking
armpit or crotch from the long trip -- and now the
stampede for the outlandishly noisy baggage carousel:
sounds like storm troopers tramping on a thin tin
roof.)
     Friday night the building in which the firm
"offices" was again closed down for repairs, so I'm
coming in for a regular workday tonight instead (except
I may take a sick day if the workload turns out to be
too heavy -- tomorrow dayscoper Doris returns from
vacation and we're back to full post-Cathy strength and
I figure why not let old Turkey deal with it -- since
I'm history as an employee and still have a full week of
sick leave to use and it being all but unthinkable the
firm would compensate me for what leave I don't use).
     Friday morning, since I knew I'd be off that night
owing to the building repairs, I stayed in town late to
run various endgame errands. These included closing my
old bank account (same one I opened when D and I first
got to town, though the bank itself has mutated several
times in both name and ownership) -- doing this because

another outfit offers a bank-machine-only account with
no monthly charges, thereby saving me seventy bucks a
year. And a stop at the city business offices to check
into the cost of a license for Jyzer Ink. It's sixty-
five dollars annually, and I'll have to pay the full
sixty-five just to cover November and December, then
pony up another sixty-five for next year.

Waiting room nearly empty now. But the continental
itself is still here, still rumbling and wheezing and
humming in place, shivering slightly from time to time
like a horse (iron) after a long gallop. Ninety minutes
until the next train is due in, that one a mere regional,
and it too is on schedule according to the board. But
by then I'll be long gone.

With Doris out it's been a bad two weeks for doing
my own work at the office. One frantic night after
another. How shamelessly elated I am not to be staying
on as part of a two-scoper day crew trying to cope over
the long term with such a heavy workload. If it holds
at anything like the present level they'll be
overwhelmed. In that case what would happen? Would the
firm call the "invaluable" nightscoper back in to do
some contract work? Not likely, especially with the
rates he's planning to post (this week he'll be making
up a scale). Would they hire someone else? Could be,
but it probably wouldn't work out. And partner Fran
wants that salary money to buy more powerful machines --
so they can upgrade to whatever the latest fancy
software is and thus do more real-time reporting, which
just happens to be Fran's own specialty (and no one
else's in the firm). Most likely the partners would try
to convince more reporters to do their own scoping,
perhaps dangling some financial incentives to get them
moving. Hard to say how this would affect me, contempo
G, sole-prop.-to-be of Jyzer Ink, if at all. Could get
more page-rate work, could get less. (For example,
another nickle or dime per page might convince reporter
Verna to do her own scoping rather than use me.)

It'll probably be several months before a clear
picture of the new setup emerges. Meanwhile I must get

myself moving on "Jyzer" again no matter what. This may
be my last big chance for a long, long time.

Hopefully D won't need to look for a job. But if
Verna goes to self-scoping we'll have no choice. D of
course is far from delighted with the prospect. No
retro self-sacrificing romantic she, especially not when
it comes to hiring herself out for hard labor so her
howler zen-hub can scratch out still more of his wacky
JIFT. What would she do if things got so bad she had to
take on two jobs? I asked that very question. Her
reply: "Call in --," citing the name of the notorious
"doctor of death" who's leading the national campaign
to legalize doc-administered mercy killings.

*

-- A mutterer's locked in one of the station men's-
room stalls. Deep slurred whiskey voice. I could make
out only a few words: "jail," "piss," "cigarette." He
appeared to be addressing my shoes beneath the partition
as I stood at the urinal. (The coin-lock gate outside
the men's room isn't in use at the moment. One or two
mutterers are tolerable, apparently; the gate seems to
be for when they, or we, threaten to overrun the place,
which we sometimes do. This part of town is prime hobo
turf. Last night's newly tabloidized news at eleven led
with the immolation of two drifters as they slept on a
loading dock about three blocks due west from where I
now sit -- doused those dudes with gasoline and set
them afire. Culprit(s) still on the loose.)

-- This right here being the newly tabloidized
Channel Jyze at Nine. (8:55 to be precise, if the
interior station clock is right, which is doubtful.)

Health update for me? Nah, not this time. (There
goes the cooled-down continental, headed for the yard.)
I'm holding. "Life is a holding action" -- corollary of
"stay against confusion" -- or should that be "contusion"
since it's what I actually wrote?

D did let her parents know my job ax has fallen. A
lot depends on how they react, especially next spring.
Will the howler be back on his feet by then? It's not
too likely. They have no conception what an out-and-out

115

miracle it is he's been able to keep their fragile-
healthed daughter in vittles and unitards all these
years. Sometimes he can scarcely believe it himself.
(Shamelessly spoiled and adored only child too.
Shouldn't fail to mention such highly relevant facts.)
     The regional's now delayed an hour. No big problem
for anyone sitting here since the jyzer has become it,
the only sitter remaining in the entire waiting room,
not counting the men's-room mutterer and the station
crew, all currently hidden from view. (Another freight
rolling through -- or no, just a brace of switch engines
merrily deadheading toward the docks.)
     How sick am I tonight? I'll soon find out. If
sick enough I'll be able to catch up on sleep before
going home. Two Sunday nights left for typing up the
end of the spree of '87-88 and reprinting the corrected
protojyze from the many-paged year of the second major
breakup with Lady S and six months later the arrival of
Lady V on the romance scene. After I go to page rate
I'll have to be much more cautious about using the
office machines for this kind of stuff, even an
occasional few pages. The sanction, however, has not
yet been officially revoked.
     Some illuminating thoughts about "Howler" this
week. Probably it's my most commercially promising
manuscript of them all. If I can't get off the dime on
"Jyzer" I might have to shove "Howler" ahead of it. And
"Notes on Ending with R" (who's really V) would come
right after that. Then "Viridescence."
     Very soon all this will no longer be merely
theoretical.

4.

     Same time, same train station, one week later.
     But what a week. We dodged two bullets, the two
baddest bullets.

Crisis over. Now the period of change begins.

First act of the new era: knock madly on wood. Pew wood, no less. Or pewlike.

(That's the usual continental humming out there. This time I'm right by the door and so can almost reach out and stroke the beast. It arrived an hour late; as I came walking up, late myself, a line of private cars and taxis was pulling out of the parking lot. And up above, a huge harvest moon for a moment seemed to fasten a fifth face on the clock tower -- froze me on the spot, that voluptuous sight did -- or from my perspective it seemed a third face, rather, two slightly elliptical and one, the moon itself, just about perfectly spherical although no less wrong on the time than the other two, except maybe by the lunar calendar. And I wouldn't bet on that either.)

How did it happen? I worked up a written plea for reporter Verna saying I needed to know, was I her scoperman or not. And more important I told her I'd finally figured out how to do the math and she would come out at least nine cents ahead per page if she paid me eighty (and this was true, a truthful claim, and I offered to guarantee it in writing).

For the next day I was biting my nails and resigned to doing so for much longer. But the following night at the office when I opened the safe containing the grand-jury jobs (always the first task after firing up my machine) there it was, the Word, a note from Verna of a single sentence now burned into my memory like a line of great poetry: "Eighty cents is fine, as long as it's eighty cents to me." -- And eighty cents to her it is! (And ten cents to the firm, so seventy cents to Jyzer Ink. And that's still almost half again what I'd been prepared to accept.)

(A big hiss and the continental's hum lowers by about two-thirds, both in volume and pitch. -- Regional again running on time this week, by the way, I'll note, but the second continental's two hours late. The third, tomorrow morning's Mentokan, is six hours late.)

So whoopee! -- Though I didn't feel as good as I

thought I should. Didn't then or the next day or even Thursday or even Thursday night when D leaned in to wake me up with the words "Benign. It's benign" -- though of course the relief on that was tremendous, bullet number two whizzing harmlessly by.

So why haven't I been feeling better? All week I've been puzzling about this. All right, good news takes a while to sink in. Unknowns still abound, and not just those regarding the nuts and bolts of the new work regime. Will D and I have to move out in the spring? Is she pregnant? And of course: can I get "Jyzer" written? And to be sure all the usual bedrock existential stuff. Will my mother and the U's keep on surviving? Will my own health hold up? -- But even acknowledging all this I'm still puzzled. A dark hum of worry.

To hell with it then? Yes. Jyze on.

(The usual groans of dismay as people straggle up to check the board. Meanwhile a railroad worker closes and locks door No. 1 a few feet to my left. A moment ago she was out there zipping around with scary nonchalance -- doing wheelies almost -- on a seemingly souped-up electric baggage cart that was completely empty except for her.)

By sheer coincidence the next morning after I found Verna's epochal one-line note the phone rang at the office at 5:55 and it was partner Fran. Yes, the Master herself. First spoken communication between us since before the crisis began. Her shit-eating "heh heh." She knows what a bastard she's been. She also knows she's been outmaneuvered and she's obviously not happy about it, and that's tough. I'm just sorry I can't be more direct with her. But better not to antagonize her further. As much as possible I'll be trying to keep a low profile at the office.

She said she was wondering why I hadn't answered her previous letter. "You mean the one confirming I was RIF'd?" Heh heh. Yeah, that one. "The one also saying the numbers on your proposal for contract scoping were a bit high." Oh-ho, that one, right. -- So I said I'd only just now found out that Verna and Naomi wanted to go ahead with the page-rate deal and I'd be getting back to her soon with a revised contract-scoping rate chart, "reductions for bulk hours and long-term notice and all kinds of exciting stuff." "Sounds good," she said, of course not meaning it since I'd written the same in my letter containing the rates she was now saying she thought should be lower. -- And I had to dash for the ferry. Bye. P.S.: Hope I never have to talk with you again, Fran. (No doubt she felt the same way.)

Tomorrow night I'll work up the new chart for her. I'm planning to lower my "standard rate" by fifty cents, from $17.50 to $17.00, but it'll still be way higher than she'll like. Too bad. Actually I hope they don't use me at all on a contract basis. I'll also be raising my rate to $18.00 on same-day notice. Let them scream. Fact is, as noted before, they should be paying me somewhere between $17.50 and $18.00 if the rate's to match the sum of my current salary plus the value of my soon-to-be-lost benefits. I'll also offer them even lower rates for a one-year contract for steady part-time hours (one or two nights a week) and for bulk hours, i.e. forty-hour blocks for which they give me notice the previous month (filling in for a vacationing dayscoper, say). The one-year contract hours (at $16.00) I know they'll reject because in effect they've already done so; I mean that's basically what my termination is all about. The bulk hours (at $16.50) they may or may not use me for but it's not likely to happen anytime soon because Doris and Amy won't be taking any more vacation until next summer. Truth is I'm offering these rates just so I can put some lower numbers on the chart and then say, "Well, you want to save money, here's how."

(And suddenly after all this time, out rolls the empty first continental facing the opposite direction from usual. Did it get a rush-job call? That'll be $18,000 an hour, thank you. Business is business and that's just how it is. -- And we're into a long quiet time now here at the terminal where most lines end. -- At least the place is warm. I started wearing my green jacket this week. Probably in another month or so, six weeks, the black winter coat. Always look forward to that because I like that coat. I'm bad in that coat. Yeah. Even Lady U says so.)

   -- As it turned out, Nightscoper G, newly superannuated version, didn't take those sick days early last week, but once the good news came in at midweek he was emboldened to do so after all. Worked half nights Wednesday and Thursday and didn't go in at all Friday. Focused on proofing, cleaning, getting ready for the big changeover to Jyzer Ink, i.e., myself as independent contractor and sole proprietor.

   -- Quiet talk in the train station. Distant whistle, the first of the night, right at the moment of writing "train" in the previous sentence as if I had pressed a button with the J-stick. Hums of vending machines and unidentifiable hidden motors meanwhile harmonizing almost like a barbershop quartet and possibly those big fluorescent squares high overhead pitching in as well with an ultra-high tenor to make it a quintet (for sure they're at least crackling).

   -- This being the week of Mother's trip to the M. zone. This weekend she's in Lahontan, home city of her teen years and early twenties, city where she met Dad, city of my birth; tonight she's staying (with Jim Q.) at the very inn where I stayed almost exactly a year ago because she and Dad used to bivouac there when they attended football games or visited brothers Rob and Jeff during their college years. Last night she and Jim put up at Jeff's "farmette" twenty miles outside of town, again as I did a year ago. Fine place: an old farmhouse that the talented craftsman Jeff's slowly fixing up amid lots of ramshackle outbuildings including a classic red wooden dairy barn and a silo, stately trees, rolling hills and cornfields, Holsteins grazing in pastures -- the authentic heartland pastoral scene par excellence (though subdivision developments are crowding in just out of sight on all sides and Jeff himself is helping to build one of them as a carpenter).

   Distant, I mean truly distant bass line, the evil

dictator of a Mideast nation feints as if to make
another grab for another Mideast nation; the U.S., self-
appointed boss of the world, furiously flings troops and
planes. More flinging of same at that small Caribbean
nation mentioned earlier that's dared to show a little
feisty spirit. Same old knuckle-under-or-else U.S.
demands, though as of yet, this round, they've led to no
bloodshed that I know of. Kids starving to death by the
tens of thousands in that first Mideast nation mentioned
above, yes, but that's simply "the cost of refusing to
do business our way" -- that is, the "sanctions" part.
Go along to get along and we won't starve your kids or
blast you to smithereens, that's the deal, a/k/a "the
Washington Consensus," the penalty section thereof.
Obviously the media have assiduously determined that
everyone everywhere has signed on to this deal or
otherwise they, the media, wouldn't so smugly be calling
it "the Washington Consensus." Or are they merely
saying everyone in Washington agrees on it (which of
course would also be a lie). -- And whose media is
this? Why, it's our media! Waddaya know!

(Doors swing open and stay propped that way, a
blast of cold air: it's the ho-hum regional rolling in.
Not yet but in a few minutes.)

-- And so begins my last week of work at the
office. Full-time work as an employee, this is. And
here's hoping it's also my last week of full-time work
ever, anywhere, as an employee or for that matter as an
independent contractor or vendor or sole proprietor or
entrepreneur or whatever's the going glamorized term.
But none of these last-named five is exactly a slam
dunk.

What plans for this important week? None to speak
of. Survive it. Print up what truly should be the last
two reams of protojyze, their focus on the high era with
Lady S; type up the last fifty pages of the spree (which
came to an end six years ago last month, by the way, and
focused to an almost demented degree, I can say now, on
the deteriorating relations between me and Lady U which
would soon inspire us to try country living -- with her

parents' indispensable help -- in fact it was their
suggestion). Meanwhile spend carefully because the next
paycheck from the firm will be my last.

-- And here they are, regional types entering.
Emphatically not continental people. The regional train
itself has pulled in several tracks over, a low-status
spur. A janitor in blue jumpsuit wants to "get the butt
under your seat." It's not my butt, I let her know, the
one down there on the floor. She sweeps it up without
comment but I can tell she's skeptical about my
assertion and probably not too happy she used the word
"butt" in the first place. (Now a heavy freight's
rolling by behind the regional, moving wheels visible
under stationary cars, lights flashing, bells clanging,
heavy rumble. Big doings here! Floor doesn't shake,
doesn't tilt, doesn't do anything, but should do all
that and more.)

So fine. Doggone. It is. Jyze heaven here.

-- But can't linger forever. In fact -- begone
behind this last one-sentence inky jyze miniburst.
Scoot!

5.

End of the line. This is it, the de facto last
night. And I'm right here, in the larger of the two
office conference rooms. Dark and stormy night out
there (a couple-three weeks back the curtain banged down
on summer and it's been rainy, blustery, cold ever
since). No one else around.

Other than the nightscoper's own declaration, any
overt sign it's his last night on the job? Not a one.
Opposite of a fine howdayado. Where's the brass band?
Where's the champagne and the cake with the stripper
popping out? Some kind of gratitude for fifteen years'
top-of-the-line service. Yeah.

No second white envelope either (or it would be
more like the fourth, if I'm right). I expected one and

was prepared to milk it for all it was worth in these
pages. (Why not -- because real-life stories are few
and far between for this jyzer in recent years and here
one is, at least relatively speaking: the naked city
finally coughing one up just for me. -- As noted
previously, no doubt. "Second verse, a whole lot like
the first.")

A week ago last night the contract-scoping rate
chart for partner Fran came into being. I left it on
her desk along with an authentically businesslike cover
letter. Cackled over it -- figured aha and now the trap
snaps shut. Next day I was gloating less, thinking the
chart had gone maybe a bit too far, suddenly fearful the
whole page-rate deal would blow up in Jyzer Ink's face
(in the very same way I'd been thinking Fran's decision
to RIF the nightscoper had blown up in her face).

Since then not a word from anyone. Early Friday
a.m. this jyzer, now seriously worrying, jotted a brief
note in the office log saying he'd henceforth be going
over to page rate. Dayscoper Doris didn't bother to
initial it to show she'd read it, though under
longstanding protocol she's supposed to. A little
message right there, I'd say, from old Turkey to the
soon-to-be-ex Jyzelby. No doubt just the first of many.
"Oop-oop-a-doop, you're outta the loop."

(And there goes the phone again. Someone's trying
hard to reach someone. Could be almost anyone calling
almost anyone but from the persistence I'd guess it's
ol' Mom trying to reach -- me, yeah. I mailed her a
card this morning so maybe I'll just let the rings go
unanswered for now. I'm supposed to be in the office
for only four hours tonight and that means once again I
can get away with acting as if I'm not here yet -- it's
about eleven -- even if the caller's one of the partners.
-- And the ringing has continued through most of this
paragraph and is still going on now. -- Just stopped.
-- The problem being enough scoping work awaits me that
getting into a long talk with Mom would mean I couldn't
do my jyze bit. And tonight jyze comes first.) (And
there it goes again, the phone. It can't be D because

she always gives the two-ring signal first.)
     And so: do I still have the page-rate part-time
job? I'm assuming so. Even though I'm officially on
vacation starting tomorrow and then terminated as of
next Monday (nice to go out for good on All Hallow's
Eve), I'm planning to come in Thursday night, seventy-
two hours from now, to begin grand-jury page-rate work
under the auspices of Jyzer Ink. (The phone's ringing
again.) Tomorrow morning I'll be applying for my
official business license under that name. But...who
knows what'll actually be happening.
     That's the thing. That hum of worry, it continues
because the future is full of unknowns. No shit Dick
Tracy! But "job security" is gone. At any moment,
whooom, Jyzer Ink could go kablooey, maybe even before
it officially exists. Can't count on anything. Thus
this manic state. Might be in luck with my change of
employment status, might be out of luck.
     (Office doors open and I, this G, freeze. But it's
only the janitor. Him I've even been expecting.
Industrial vacuum cleaner starts up with the decibels of
a moon rocket. He's probably surprised I'm not hunched
over bleary-eyed in my usual spot in front of the screen.
Latino guy, little or no English, always wearing
headphones and listening to salsa or whatever (it's
Latin music anyway I know) -- but friendly. He's been
around close to a year -- longest-reigning janitor of my
entire stint with the firm except for Jane at the
previous building who beat the impossible odds and rose
to supervisor. But she's a howler. And to this day I
sometimes see her taking a break outside that building,
pluming cigarette smoke like an old ten-wheel steam
engine, as I walk by on my way up here.)
     (And down at the ferry terminal Ray the newspaper
delivery guy, also a howler, he who rolls the cart
groaning with papers aboard the ferry at the same time I
usually get on, he's counting down to retirement in
perfect synchrony with my own RIF countdown: he's outta
there as of Halloween. Every day he's crowing "Just ten
more days," "Just seven more days" -- and of course

that's me too. Except I'm not crowing or even
mentioning my new status on the ferry.)
     And at home the workers finish up with the back
door, the attic room, the roof vents, the bathroom
heater, the bedroom ceiling. "We're sliding into
poverty but at least the bedroom ceiling no longer
sags." All this is part of the sprucing-up effort to
make the house salable, and we're just not going to
worry about that right now. Not give it a single
additional thought. (But Papa U has kindly insisted we
cut back or suspend our monthly two-hundred-dollar
payments on the loan he provided so we could buy the
wagon.) (And the registration renewal bill on D's old
car arrived: that one we'll have to let go. Insurance
costs are just too much. Henceforth it will sit in the
garage unregistered. At age nineteen it's not worth the
trouble of trying to sell it.) (To be strictly accurate
it's not a garage it's sitting in, it's a carport, open
at both ends, also new and also part of the sprucing-up
effort.)
     "So what?" to all this? Right. Just trying to
work in a few hard details. (Another one: a new cat
shows up, orange, bushy tail that looks just like a
fox's except it quivers in the straight-up position if
you touch it, and this cat bounces around in an odd way
so D's calling him Hoppy; and now he's another mouth to
feed and we're worried about the additional expense.
-- But with four "outside cats" already issued lifetime
meal tickets, what's one more? And of course Fred the
inside cat lives like a king, no way any of his daily
expenses can be cut back even if it means D and I start
boiling roots from the wetland for our own meals -- that
being a running poverty joke, of which we've got quite a
few now, no doubt in part to defuse tensions -- and pray
tell why else? -- So just drop all this.)
     -- But manic. Which means exciting moments too.
     -- This meanwhile being World Series time in the
year of no baseball and thus the air of unreality
heightens further. If the Great USAn Pastime can be
canceled almost without notice, what can they do with

all our miserable little individual games and scams?
    Still pounding rain, still wind. Roar of a bus on
the street far below. No phone ringing for the past
page or maybe slightly more. (Brother Rob was supposed
to be calling too but he wouldn't ring that long. Of
course someone could be defunct or dead -- all kinds of
ghastly possibilities. But no need to think about those
now. And lord knows they're always about to dial you up
anyway.)
    So this is it. Last night at the old stand. Last
jyze bulletin from the RIF'd zone. To be sure I'll be
back, and in just three days, but it won't be the same.
Close of an era. Cusp. Divide. Sea change.
    And nothing more to say about it? So it seems.
Just sitting here frowning. What else? -- Fear of my
own obsolescence, I guess. The high working life may be
ending right here. Probably the closest I'll ever come
to having a career. The sidetrack shunt. Somewhat like
those Japanese salarymen who become deadwood in their
forties or fifties and suddenly find themselves raking
leaves for a zaibatsu subsidiary somewhere out in the
sticks. But here of course the zaibatsu just shows you
the door. Even the tiniest zaibatsu does. It's our
way. Without it some other country might get to be boss
of the world.
    Think about it, unemployed scum!
    (Phone again. But I'm not answering tonight except
between two a.m. and six.)
    -- And so for the last time ever (probably) in the
mainstream full-time vocational hooked-in-with-society
sense: time to get to work.
    Next time, thirty the whole damn job.

6.

    No, actually that wasn't it. That was just the de
facto it. This is the real it. And the real it is not

126

so good. Though I'll tiptoe out on a limb and say it's
also not so bad.

When is this? Bizarro fictive-like day. Demons,
fairies, nasty Rambos and Howard the Ducks and bikini'd
R2-D2s wherever you look. At the gas station a giant
talking beer can takes my money. At the home-port cafe
a witch in a peaked cap with silver tinsel for hair
serves my coffee. As I turn into our road the old green
pickup heading out is driven by a clown in full costume
and face paint and red spaghetti hair, a Bozo so real-
looking he might be unrecognizable were it not for the
his-and-her gun rack. All day it's like this, and of
course it's supposed to be, it's sanctioned, but then
again it's not: it's all Satan's work. I even saw a man
make exactly that claim, very irately, on the TV news at
the cafe -- and he was wearing a ten-gallon cowboy hat!

And again it's been literally storming all day.
And the clocks are all screwed up, and not just because
it's the law, though it is (fall back). Power goes out
and the scope office plunges into blackness for seventy-
some hours straight -- it's divine retribution! It's
the demons! And Ray pushes his newspaper cart around
the state ferry for the last time -- he's off to a
tropical paradise tomorrow morning -- wasting not a
single day. He's outta here. And so am I. Even more
so than I'd thought.

(And a guy sprays the White House with automatic
rifle fire. So it's tough at the top too.)

Things started going wrong on the very day they
were supposed to start going right. Thursday night I
was scheduled to inaugurate the new page-rate deal.
Tuesday I had trudged up and down various avenues in the
rain, probably five or six miles in all, to score a city
business license for Jyzer Ink (actually except for the
weather and the shoe leather it came easy). As the new-
iteration Jyzer 3.0 (real, fictive, incorporated) I
thought I was ready. The hum of worry was down to --
well, it was still the same hum but not causing me to
vibrate quite so much (and I should say a hum really is
out there; when I lie down to take a nap on the couch at

home at three a.m. I can hear it and I think it must be
the same hum that the media say millions of others are
hearing these days, a big mystery, apparently arising
from the bowels of the earth, though lately the story
seems to be fading -- maybe the hush-up is on as a
while back it was with flying saucers supposedly -- but
I heard this hum myself! And still do!) (D can't hear
it at all. She humorously suggests what I hear might be
coming from a more familiar source right on my desk: the
flock of deep-throated wooden hummingbirds.)
     -- And so. Thursday night I'm ready to go in. All
the ducks are in a row (lots of them around these days
too, real ones, mostly in V's slicing overhead, quacking
and squawking, honking when they're geese, and a large
portion of them, or so it seems, splashing down in
puddles in our yard and out in the ditches by the road)
-- and already I'm getting up at ten to four in the
afternoon every day so I'll be ready to receive a call
from the office should they want to summon me -- four to
five p.m. are the hours I'm reachable, thank you -- and
on this first day the phone does ring (admittedly I'm
not up yet but D does a good job covering for me until I
can stagger out) -- and it's dayscoper Doris. My buddy.
Sweet Turkey who still has not uttered sympathetic word
one to me about the RIF. My work colleague for more
than a decade. The sabotage queen. And Doris in
neutral voice tells me reporter Verna's called from the
courthouse and asked her, Doris, to ring me up and say I
shouldn't come in. Doris doesn't know what's up but
Verna will phone me when she drops by the office on her
way home.
     Uh-oh. Looks like a glitch. Could be bad, I warn
D. Verna the shaky one. Talented but eccentric. You
can't count on her. You know these artist types.
     (By the way, at the moment I'm holed up in one of
the new demo booths at the city ferry terminal. The
seven-twenty left a while back, the seven-fifty just
gave a warning toot prior to pulling out. Figured this
is the right place to be tonight because hereafter I
won't be able to do this -- won't have a monthly ferry

pass gaining me entree to the inside waiting area whenever I please and for as long as I please. Now I'll be switching over to ten-ride coupon books and it'll cost me a coupon every time I stick my nose in here.)

And yes the news was bad. Verna, when she called an hour later, revealed that because of the way the firm was setting up the accounting she probably wouldn't be able to use Jyzer Ink on page-rate. In essence they would be forcing her to pay J. Ink immediately and then wait four to eight weeks for the government check to come in to pay her, and as we all know she's bringing up two kids, she has house payments to make, she has a new boyfriend to keep happy, she lives from check to check. Couldn't she just carry it herself, reporter Naomi had asked her, but Naomi just doesn't understand; she, Naomi, has her husband with his big lawyer's paycheck, blah blah blah. Verna was sorry but -- but. -- And it wasn't her fault for dropping this bombshell at the last moment, she wanted me to know. Partner Una had promised her the accounting would be done in such a way that she, Verna, would not be carrying the charges; partner Fran had waited until the last moment to tell Verna they had decided it would be otherwise. Typical of the partners, Verna said (and how right she was on that one): broken promises and bad communications, with Fran the ultimate hard-nose villain as almost always.

Well, I said, how about if I just "loan" the money for the J. Ink bill right back to her, that is, let her delay paying for real until after the government check comes in? Instead of her bankrolling me, I would bankroll her.

This was mostly a bluff. Maybe I could borrow from Mother or the U's to get far enough ahead of the game to be able to do this? But it brought Verna up short. Fumble, mumble. Hadn't thought of that. Might be tax problems (for a short-term loan from me to her? Not likely). Stutter. Maybe she would look into it, ask Una or Naomi. How about if she called me back tomorrow on this because it was late, she had to get going, kids waiting to be picked up, Frank (the new boyfriend)

expecting dinner. Meanwhile I should cancel my plans to
come in that night. Hang on though. We'll see.

Then a twenty-four-hour pause before learning Verna
had sold me down the river. Left me bobbing in the
ferry backwash. So to speak! Of course I can't really
blame her for showing no loyalty or gratitude for all
those years I busted my ass for her (endangering my job
and in fact eventually losing it in part because I was
spending extra off-the-books time on her grand-jury
stuff along with Naomi's -- but then this too was part
of my strategy for keeping myself indispensable, and it
did work for a lot of years against heavy odds).

Why should Verna be loyal? This is business! We
live in Businessland! And the truth is Verna'll do
better scoping grand jury herself (because her writing's
so clean) except when it's very difficult; only then
should she pay a scoper to do it. But she knew with
me it would have to be all or nothing, or at least she
assumed that; she didn't want to be wrestling with her
conscience each week: "Will the poor guy starve if I
scope this one myself to save a few bucks?"

She couldn't bring herself to reveal the true
reason during the Friday call. But I know. And she
probably knows I know. Or maybe not. In any event I
didn't want to squawk. If business picks up down the
road she might change her mind. And I know since she's
invested in her own home transcription system (that's
the new gizmo suddenly fouling everything up for in-
office scopers everywhere) she has to justify the
expenditure by using the damn thing. So, fine. If
circumstances change don't hesitate to call, Verna. I
understand you couldn't help it. See you around, pal.

So one of the twin pillars propping up my Jyzer Ink
scheme has crumbled. Only reporter Naomi remains. And
it's not likely I'll be getting any other work from the
office. I still haven't heard a peep from the partners
on my contract-scoping rate chart. They're probably
thinking "Fuck him!" Later on I may make an effort to
show them that with benefits figured in they'd be paying
me ten to twenty percent less to work on contract than

they're currently paying the dayscopers. Trouble is
they're probably too set in their ways to believe this.
And that's just how it is and has always been with them.
Nobody disputes this. They admit it themselves when
circumstances are right and the money's rolling in:
they're just reporters, not businesspeople or tech
wizards and certainly not accountants.

Like Dad saying he's just a country boy? And him a
corporate attorney? Well, but a country boy he also
was. Neither Turtle Rapids nor Wachute is Centropolis
not to mention Megalopolis. And Una and Fran are
authentic country girls, both hailing from outbacks high
on the remoteness scale. Neither has much education or
any sophistication at all in management. But they're
not dumb, no. And come to think of it, in the instant
case they did manage to succeed in the end in dividing
the opposition (reporters Verna and Naomi) and setting
them to fighting between themselves. They did manage to
get rid of their highest-paid and longest-serving
employee without incurring any major trouble or expense,
at least so far. They brought off a nifty, almost pain-
free downsize. In the process they turned the smart-guy
nightscoper into RIF-raff.

And. And. Should I be upset? Worried? Scared
half to death? Or should I say, well, things look even
better now? Instead of going in to the city a day or
two or three every week I'll have to do that only every
other week, so I'll gain free time and yet still have
access to the office computers and printers. My
prospective income from the firm will be cut in half but
I'll have a better case to present to Employment
Security (I'm seeing them Wednesday); I should be able
to bump up the benefits from them, at least for a while.
So am I worse off or better off?

Last week after my de facto final night I bought a
deep-dish apple pie and a quart of D's favorite fancy
French vanilla ice cream on the way home and announced
upon arrival it was time for the celebration to begin.
And except for this one glitch with Verna pulling the
carpet out from under Jyzer Ink, or her half of the

carpet anyway, it's been a most excellent week. Poverty
suits me just fine as long as the wolf is not yet at the
door (though five hungry cats be lurking out there at
all times and a fifth-column sixth cat prowling and
preening inside). I even went all euphoric after what
began as a brief glimpse into my own newly reprinted
overseas protojyze turned into a heady one-day total
reimmersion. (There's some truly good shit in there,
even my sternest perfectionistic self can't deny it.)
Now I'm about to plunge back into "Jyzer" world and I do
have hopes -- oh do I.

So? It's good. Or it isn't. Maybe it's the void.
As of midnight tonight I have no health insurance and no
prospect of getting any (though we'll try to keep D's
going because she needs it for week-to-week survival
whereas I haven't seen a doctor since well before she
and I met) -- but who would be surprised if I were
diagnosed with some hideous glioblastoma or any of ten
thousand other highly expensive if not fatal maladies
let's say tomorrow? Not I. It may not be so but to me
it seems almost inevitable. To me the best I can hope
for is week-to-week sentence deferral. Sure I know
that's true for everyone. But my odds are worse than
most. They're undeniably bad. Even so I'll go on and
I'll be bursting into jyze until the end or as long as
there's a ghost of a chance of doing so.

Ghosts. Ghostly night. O Ghostly Night, the Moon
is Brightly Shining. -- But it ain't.

Meanwhile a morale booster from the U's. Sell the
house, they say -- to D's friends Marissa and Curtis if
at all possible since that would save closing costs and
at least some of the cleanup hassles; and do it while
their interest level is still high -- and then use the
proceeds, or a portion of them if it's possible to go
cheap, and buy ourselves some sort of townhouse (which D
tells me is their word for condo) and live there and
then the U family and friends will continue to have a
place to stay when they visit. And for god's sake make
it a place where the upkeep is minimal so they, the U's,
don't have to be doing it for us when they come because

they're getting too old for that.

But would there be room for my books and papers?
How about my battered pride? Swallow it again?
Probably I could do that. But should I?

(Another boat about to leave. Cop trying to arouse
a sleeping drunk two booths up. -- Now the drunk falls
to the floor, like a log rolling off a steep riverbank.
Kerplunk. Ouch. You all right, homey? But up and
shambling doorward apparently feeling no pain. -- Cop
also looks quizzically at me since I'm the only one left
in here and I've been here a long time. What am I
waiting for, the Titanic? The Ship of Fools? Ha-ha-ha!
And that's not a Keystone Kop uniform he's wearing for
Halloween. But just as I'm reaching to pull out my pass
that expires at midnight he suddenly turns and wanders
off. Meaning what? Possibly meaning it's not illegal
yet -- or at least it's tolerated -- to be drunk on
jyze. -- Corny, yeah, agreed, but that's how I'd like
to think of it. And on this extraordinary day I deserve
to have at least this one wish granted. Yes!)

-- Next mission, up to the office to pick up my
last salary paycheck. Hereafter the checks, if any,
will be made out to Jyzer Ink (I've got the temporary
license in my shirt pocket; and the "permanent" one,
good for all of sixty-six days -- which works out to a
bargain-basement price of ninety-nine cents a day --
will be coming in the mail). This incorporation of jyze
I'm not exactly proud of but it's putting the best-
possible face on things. It's a globalizing marketized
world out there and it's not just out there either, it's
right here. And not only right here outside (in the
pocket), it's right here inside, colonizing the very
heart of the jyzer, newly installed CEO of Jyzer Ink.
"Call Me Corporado."

Guess I'll get used to it. Or if there's some
other way to go my ears remain open.

The low hum of high-yield worries. (That's a
rock'n'roll pun, I like it, I'm gonna remember it, like
"Mama Got Juice.")

Is fun this. Aw heck. Springs all just about

sprung for now, I can relax like a despavined slinky
toy. Later for new tensions and finding new spav, or
new skaz maybe, as in the quasi-jyzey Russian lit form
(if I'm remembering right and spelling right too).
Meanwhile slink off into the unknown -- clown, ghost,
demon domain. "Satan's work." "It's a demon, it's a
devil, it's -- Jyzelbeelzebub!"

CHAPTER EIGHT

[Blank Jyze]

1.

    A chilly drizzly night in early dark season --
early enough that tomorrow's election day. And (or is
it but?) it's cozy down here in the ORB cafe. Epicenter
of our local lit world, or so declared an article in one
of the dailies just last week about people who write in
cafes (the reporter couldn't find anyone working on the
Great USAn Novel and made that her well-worn and rather
flimsy peg: yet another era has passed). -- In the back
corner would be cozier but two book clubs are meeting in
the area, with lots of loud talk and laughter. My usual
table is free right next to them but jyze might feel a
bit self-conscious there. Close proximity to book clubs
in high-octane action it's not ready for, now or, I'd
guess, ever.
    I'm trying to think more. Pause. Not be too hasty
or breathless, rushed, frantic. After all I've become a
man of leisure. Free time to burn. "Essays in
Idleness": here's my chance.
    -- What I forgot about last entry was the grace
period. That's what I've been in for the past week. On

both the insurance and the ferry pass the small print
revealed five extra days' grace. Even though I wasn't
covered anymore, I was. I would have no more paychecks
but I still had the funds from my last paycheck and that
itself was a kind of grace. I could still do most of
the things I normally do, although most of them I didn't
actually have to do, and didn't do. But it was sort of
good (queasily good) to know I could do them if I wanted
to. Buy a newspaper or a magazine, for example. A
vanilla softie as a special treat.

Meanwhile, under the aegis of all this grace, and
aptly enough on the Day of the Dead, the new life began.
It was a lot like the old life but lacking much of the
part of that which I most disliked. Instead of going
in to the city five or six days during the first week I
had to go in only twice, and on those occasions I had
to work fewer hours and I was paid more per hour. So
that wasn't bad at all. Reporter Naomi's two days of
grand jury came in at 337 pages. I did everything
exactly as before, but now with each page worth a
specific amount to me (eighty cents). Tonight I'm on my
way in to do finals. This will take two hours tops; the
rest of the night I'll be working on my own stuff in the
conference room.

So far so good. (And just don't pay the slightest
attention to that underlying high-yield hum.)

-- The one big event of the week, relatively
speaking, was the application for unemployment. I had
to drive over to the agency at eight a.m., finding it to
my surprise to be in the same state complex where I
scored my driver's license shortly before leaving for
the M. zone last year. The parking lot and waiting
lobby were jammed but things went smoothly enough: by
half past eleven I was out of there with the news that I
qualified for a weekly payment of $311 and those
payments could continue for thirty weeks or longer.
Three-quarters of what I make from my Jyzer Ink
"contract" with Naomi, however, will be deducted from
the $311, so it turns out to be true: I'm better off for
having been shafted by reporter Verna, because three-
quarters of what she paid me would've been deducted too

and thus I might not have qualified for benefits at all.

So what's the catch? Could be many. The firm could contest the award, try to trump something up. ES requires me to send in a form every two weeks attesting that I'm seeking work and to produce on demand the names of companies where I've applied; I could easily screw this up. Worst of all, I might be offered a job I'd have to accept. I'm allowed to reject anything that pays below the prevailing wage for in-office scopers, but what if a local firm (several of which employ reporters I've worked with before) wants to hire me as a full-time dayscoper at the prevailing rate? It's far from likely but it could happen. If it did I might go off the dole rather than accept. Better to stick with part-time work for Naomi and put Lady U to work. It's her turn for sure. But can she do it? And will she?

Got to admit this account is dullsville. For the moment everything's going well with my life but it's all so provisional and conditional and spelling out the nature of the many small weekly changes is such a chore. Yet I for one find these changes hard to ignore.

Tomorrow morning I go back for my mandatory class at Employment Security. This will take another four hours plus, travel time included. At home this weekend I put in two hours filling out required forms with the same basic info I'd already provided in filling out an almost identical set of forms at the ES office last week. All this is a pain in the neck but it's really not all that bad. The two other times in my life I've applied for unemployment, both in different states, the red tape was quite a bit worse. Computers have cut down on the paperwork and speeded things up. So yes, Virginia, there is progress (which isn't to say there's no regress -- but at least regress this week has brought me no obvious new personal fallout, so far).

For unemployment they call this the waiting period. It's the obverse of the grace period; they figure since you're still living on your last paycheck from your former job you can stretch that check out a bit and do without benefits the first week. Perfectly reasonable tight-ass slacker-hating assumption.

So here I sit. After tonight I'll have at least eight days free before I'm slated next to venture cityward. I'll be getting back to "Jyzer." I'm ready. Simple assertion. Factual or not, we'll see.

Of course I'm hoping D won't have to go to work until the ES benefits run out sometime in May or June (or maybe even later if the scoping for Naomi enables me to stretch out over a longer period the total amount I'm entitled to, as the regulations seem to imply). D, not at all surprisingly, is nursing the same hope.

Looking back, did I accomplish what I hoped to during the ten-week wind-down to the boot? Seems I did. All writings and notes are now on universal diskettes and all the targeted urjyze and early protojyze, fictive included, is proofed and reprinted and all but the last fifty pages of the spree protojyze are typed up. For the small portion of this which the firm kindly financed (unknowingly) as what I consider to be a form of severance pay, I say much obliged, partners Una and Fran. -- Neither of whom ever bothered to say a word to me about my departure as an employee, the one and only casualty of the RIF they had supposedly so "agonized" over. I'm still amazed. Not even a card expressing thanks for the decade and a half.

It's hard to let all this go. I guess it'll eventually decamp on its own. The slow fade. Meanwhile I'll try to enjoy being sullen. I mean I'm not this way all the time; quite often I'm ecstatic. "Love this pinch!" D and I dance around the kitchen and nerf boisterously in the basement. But in these pages tonight something seems to be grumping me out.

Could try to fit things into the larger picture. Corporate downsizing and rightsizing (so-called), nasty mood of the working classes, anger at government in general which will result in the moderate in-party bums being tossed out in the elections tomorrow (if predictions hold) only to be replaced by far worse right-wing out-party bums -- but I have no heart for taking on such a task. Globalization of raw U.S.-style

dog-eat-doggism, flight of jobs overseas, disruptions
caused by massive technological change. Obsolete
traditional morals failing, conservative religious
outrage, immigrants and illegal aliens (so-called) under
attack -- it's all dull normal these days and it's all
downright disgusting: USA thrashing clumsily, unable to
come to grips with the complicated new post-Cold War
world (complicated compared to the halcyon post-World
War II era when most of the rest of the industrial world
was in ruins and the Evil Empire provided a clear-cut
enemy and the idea of unending material progress was not
yet widely known to be in serious ecological question to
say nothing of being totally discredited as it is now,
making all the other stuff look relatively minor).
     But no. I don't want to get into the big picture
in any way more detailed than that. At this point it's
enough to sneak a glance at it from time to time through
a kind of political eclipse box -- knowing, however,
chances are very high that this particular darkening
will prove to be long-running and quite possibly total.
     One other event of sorts. Brother Rob finally
called. I wasn't home at the time but he and D chatted
a bit. He passed along some news that may be very bad:
Mother's seeing a doctor about internal bleeding she
noticed after or perhaps during her Mentoka trip with
Jim Q. So another health crisis. We're all highly
aware that any one of these, or any combo, could be her
last. (No doubt this explains why I haven't heard from
her since her Lahontan letter of several weeks ago. She
figures I've gone through enough lately; doesn't want to
burden me unnecessarily.)
     Gloom and doom. Yes! Stare it down! Ride it!
See how far it can throw you this time! Cheer if it's a
new record but also if it's not!
     (We've got a local celebrity here tonight, the
lesbian who beat the U.S. Army. A long row of mostly
female couples now filing out after a final burst of
applause that grew into a lengthy standing ovation.
Rarely have I seen a straighter-looking bunch at a
reading here: could almost be the temperance union of a

century ago in an updated version of super-sedate garb.
Nonetheless this woman is likewise one of my own heroes
of the moment.)
      -- Pause to think. Such excellent sobriety, I've
just got to be self-impressed. Can't be any doubt I'll
be catapulting off this strictly minor trauma in the
wondrous year of jyzeburst. -- Or if doubt, surmount.
      Reminding. In a week of storms and cold suddenly a
glorious clear day and the mountains to the west pop
back out and since we've seen them last they've turned a
dazzling white. And not just the caps; the scarves and
the great maxicoats too, down almost to ankle level.
Always a glorious moment and it doesn't happen every
year either; usually the snow levels slowly creep down.
      So this is uplifting, yes? Soon out will hoof
Maria R. and the Adorables with "Doe a Deer"?
      Grump and gripe. Go right ahead and wallow in it
you foul-mouthed old jyze-humping reprobate you. This
post-RIF buffeting must come to an end anyway. It's not
even intolerable. It's not even unentertaining if you
play it right, though maybe only in the writing and not
the living or the reading. (And mostly you are not
playing it right and you know it, so stop. For now.)

2.

      Blank. Blank is what you go to after the grace
period ends. The blank period.
      The shed heater is grinding away in its strange
cyclical grind, spasming out the therms. Outside the
windows the day is gray and damp and the woods are
wearing a raggedy yellow cloak -- or mostly it's this
bigleaf maple right here. The one with leaves the size,
even almost the shape and color, of flattened baseball
mitts. A sodden carpet of them I trod just moments ago
to fetch the shed key from its hiding place in the eaves
on the woods side (the tip of its hook visible from here

through the double windows, just to the left of the
faintly fluttering "Jyzer Ink" business license, the
"permanent" one that's good for all of two months,
thumb-tacked to the window centerpost inside).
    "From the desk of the hummingbird whirligigs."
(And rubber stamps. And old books. And wooden boxes.
And parrot molas. And art pins, postage stamps,
decorator pens, ink bottles, public-market newsstand
calendars, Mentoka memorabilia -- and then there's the
real clutter.)
    -- And me the newly official sole prop. in an
authentic three-day stubble along with muddied black
sweatpants and knee-high brown rubber barn boots and
gray hooded sweatshirt above stinky layered heavy long-
sleeve henleys. Trudging up in the rain I was surprised
to hear the sound of the workaday world roaring over
from the freeway (actually more a muttering by the time
it filters through half a mile of forest, though
vivified with an occasional pachydermic truck horn-
blare). "Hey, I'm not part of that anymore," I observed
out loud. With neither elation nor sorrow. "Just how
it is." Or for the most part anyway. That's what this
license here really says, the fine print.
    Of course I'm not so happy about the consequences.
The worries and unknowns are too numerous. I have to be
thinking about them way too much. Can't just go all
oblivious (much as I might like to -- but only might,
because obliviousness has never been my game -- or at
least not intentionally). (Shed roof creaking, which it
does a lot -- usually just owing to the wind, somehow,
though once in a while a small furry animal's creeping
around up there, or birds, big ones, crows most likely,
if not ravens or, lately, if only in fantasy, vultures,
flapping and cackling and licking their beaks.) (And
drips streaking down from the eaves, I watch and every
now and then a falling maple bigleaf catches my eye --
flapping down looking less like a baseball mitt now and
more like a starfish galumphing underwater.)
    Fractured style today, more so than usual? (Shift
feet to rest left atop right, sole of left facing heater

vent -- whereas before right rode atop left. Since
we've morphed into Jyzer Ink world headquarters up
here the floor seems colder than ever -- need I say?)
     The latest missive from Employment Security appears
to imply the firm is contesting my claim. Or is this
form letter merely telling me my claim is being examined
as all claims are examined during the "waiting week"?
The phrasing's ambiguous; no way to be sure what it
means. Don't want to call to ask; that could take hours
and likely be futile anyway because the employees at ES
probably don't know what's going on themselves unless
you miraculously connect with just the right person.
The first check's due to arrive late this week or early
next; then maybe I'll learn more.
     Or of course the partners could be hitting the
roof. What ES duns from them in order to pay me will
put a big crimp in Fran's plan to upgrade the computer
system. Would the firm trump up something against me to
try to get out of paying? Something declaring, say, I
was fired for cause, not let go because they wanted the
money from my salary for a computer upgrade? In which
case I would become ineligible for benefits? They
might. Let's face it. Fran especially is not so
scrupulous. In her view the firm's very existence is in
jeopardy and therefore unscrupulousness could easily be
the order of the day. Or just out of pure spite she
might ban me from the premises while I'm squeezing the
firm for the unemployment dole; and since I'm required
to be in the firm's certified "secure" office to work on
government jobs, I'd be unable to do reporter Naomi's
scoping. (Even though sandbagging me this way would
increase the amount the firm would be required to pay me
through ES -- and now the firm would be getting nothing
at all in return for it. If the partners were smart
about it they would offer me more work, up to the ES
cutoff, because in effect they'd be getting it for free
or at greatly reduced rates.) -- Are they smart this
way? Are they spiteful this way? Stay tuned.
     Often I think I might be psychically better off
just dropping the Jyzer Ink scheme and finding some

other line of work. To hell with the firm. To be sure
this is what the whole unemployment system is designed
to make you think and do. But that doesn't mean it
might not be the better course. I hate the charade of
pretending I'm looking for a job -- and dread being
found out (that I'm not seriously looking) (for
something that almost certainly doesn't exist!) and
being forced to repay whatever I get from them. Were
some long-term stability attainable in doing so I might
prefer to take most any old scuzz job.

     Not quite yet though. Let's hang on and see what
happens.

     (Just turned the heater down to medium. Now the
vibrato grind is gone and so is the faint fluttering of
the business license. "Post conspicuously," it warns.
I figure right between the eyes -- if only the jyzer's
eyes and no one else's -- is conspicuous enough.)

     Also I can hope D will find a half-decent scuzz job
of her own. Then with the proceeds from that plus my
dollop from Naomi we'd just be able to squeeze by and
wouldn't even need unemployment benefits (though of
course I wouldn't give them up for that reason alone).

     And she's looking. Applied for a clerk position at
a camera shop this week, but she knows nothing about
cameras. (A fun day as we worked up her resume. A born
speller in English she ain't either. -- "But better
than F. Scott Fitzgerald! You said so yourself! It was
the first good thing anyone's ever said about my
spelling! That's when I knew you were a suitor to be
reckoned with!") Clerk in a health-food or vitamin
store is another one she could go for. Meanwhile she's
turning a little testy about things that up until
recently didn't seem to bother her at all. There will
be frictions, yes. But I figure we can handle them.

     (Lots of moss on that bigleaf maple -- I hadn't
noticed before. Now I have time for whole new
categories of noticing. -- Yesterday I used Andy's old
twelve-foot pole-mounted picker to strip scores of
rotting apples from the upper branches of the trees near
the carport. Tossed them on the ground, and within an

hour the deer (same family, minus one fawn, that denuded
the middle and lower branches) had somehow sniffed them
out from afar and were nibbling away at them -- and
within fifteen feet of our back door. Then Captain
Brick's "Filipina Dreamgirl" wife Jenny whom we rarely
see up close because she's supposedly so shy, she
likewise suddenly appeared and crept halfway up our
driveway in her own fawnlike way to snap photos of the
scene. Before now no one had ever known Brick to let
her leave the house unescorted. And in a form-fitting
camo hunting outfit, no less. And no more.)

Meanwhile I'm living in dread of a call from or
about Mother. I'm already on a kind of deathwatch.
Nothing I can do except try to be mentally prepared.

(I've turned sideways in search of better elbow
support -- writing lengthwise down the desktop because
the back part just beneath the windowsill is so
cluttered -- and now I find myself face-to-face with the
really real clutter. It's my shelf of personal papers:
correspondence, documents, etc. My life, right here.
Or one perspective on it I should say, since the
writings and the photo albums ride the other side of the
very same shelf. And that's it, all the G's. "The
Jyzer as All the Letter G's." "Nachlass." That is,
what's left when you factor in mortality -- meaning
take the beating heart out of it.)

This is not really jyzing. It's more like moping.
Or can jyze take on a legitimate mope dimension? Indeed
can anything be truly human that lacks a mope dimension?

Blank, as the poet said, or might've, on closer
view reveals a screen of fine-grained mope. Every grain
is itself a series of pixels or motes of mope, fractal
style.

But this shed I'll miss. This I love. This means
a great deal. Someday perhaps I'll try to write about
it in depth, an updated version of an old Japanese
classic to be called "The Ten by Twelve Foot Shed" --
noting that the original was written eight centuries ago
by another grudging urban exile of sorts. (It's always
in the back of my mind: how I'd like to go out from

"this fleeting/floating world.") (Of course it could
be that's what I'm doing with these words right now or
at any time. Better, surely, though, to think
otherwise.) (As another bigleaf flumps down, this one
impersonating a giant cherry blossom. A crinkly brown
one for a change. -- And another. And another!
Almost like the sorcerer's apprentice scattering rags!)

     That unemployment class on Tuesday was a travesty
and a heartbreaker. The room was packed and every face
grim. More forms to fill in. A long spiel delivered
listlessly by an ES staffer, all of it self-evident
stuff already spelled out in mind-numbing detail in
various manuals and handouts. Then a jarringly upbeat
video about job-hunting with a cheesy rock band booming
out musical transitions between boosterish speeches and
hokey staged job-interview scenes. No vomit bags were
provided. (Nor was a single penny of the employers'
tax money wasted on hiring real actors.)

     Otherwise I've scarcely gotten out of the house.
A few trips to the town post office and that's it. The
big excitement: in the muddy yard two or three houses
to the south of the post office on the lagoon side a
black-and-brown hog was massively a-wallow, something
like a hippo grazing in a shallow marsh. By my estimate
at least a quarter ton of hog. I hurried to fetch D
from the post office just so she could take a gander at
it -- or poke the pig while it was still in the poke --
and by the time we got back it had vanished. Never has
shown up again. And no place it could have gone in that
short period other than inside the house. For a
butchering maybe, or maybe not. Maybe just chillin'.

     -- Beyond this the nature of the "otherwise" has
been strictly blank. I'm catching up on my reading.
I'm jumping around in the utility room. I'm schmoozing
with this or that bundle of facts. I'm thinking. I'm
scheming. I'm working up to the big "Jyzer" restart
which should be happening any day now. My charge isn't
quite high enough yet, that's all. But it's building.

     Next on today's agenda: sleep. Got to be up by
four p.m. in case the phone rings. Got to figure out

some way to deal with the job-hunting charade. Got to
write a couple of letters. Got to be moving beyond the
blank now.

3.

     Back where jyze first burst upon the scene. "The
library" when the U's aren't here to claim it as a guest
room. And to my surprise I find just about everything
in the room stacked on the couch. The floor's cleared
for action! (Or for cleaning maybe. And most likely
I'll turn out to be the designated cleaner, though we
haven't discussed this yet, the lady and I.)
     Radio's unplugged. That way power outages don't
damage it. Or is that just a myth? In any event when I
reinsert the plug it's still jazz I hear. "Got my love
to keep me warm": the lyrics warbling out right now.
     But this floor is cold. Almost as bad as the shed
floor. Every hour or two all night long I'm supposed to
be flushing toilets and running the hot water to keep
the pipes from freezing. Or so it's been decreed. And
I'm doing it too, and will keep doing it, supposing I
don't crash. Which I will do (also) at some point, and
probably one not too far off. But certainly for no more
than two hours tops, so I'm pretty sure the pipes will
be okay.
     First I'll say it's good to be getting back to jyze
origins because I think I'm ready to do some hardcore
up-from-nothingness jyzing. (Pause to tuck in my triply
layered henleys in back where my odd seated posture,
sidesaddle sort of, left flank propped against couch,
legs and hips angled under coffee table, caused the
henleys to pull out at the waist -- a frigid draft
shooting straight up my spinal ravine.)
     -- Of course all's still hanging by a thread.
Until last Thursday I wasn't even sure I'd be
provisionally awarded unemployment. But that day the

first check arrived (for $297, after they deducted
three-quarters of the proceeds from my two hours of
work for reporter Naomi the previous week). In the same
mail Jyzer Ink's first check of the new era, or any era,
came in from the office (for $229, covering two weeks).
So the wolves had to retreat from the door, though not
without snarling. They'd be back, the snarls said.
Maybe soon. Watch your back. Watch everything.

Is the firm contesting the award? The Employment
Security letter seemingly implying this hasn't been
superseded. So maybe they are. Maybe I'll be booted
off the dole and told I must repay any checks I've
received. (In which case I'll appeal and should win.
But that doesn't mean it'll happen. So far lifetime I'm
batting .500 on unemployment appeals, one for two.)

This week I'll be sending off a batch of job
inquiry letters to reporter firms in other states. I'll
also try to come up with a way to apply for government
jobs. In both of these areas Employment Security opens
a big loophole: you're not required to go in for an
interview. The ES apparatchik told us so himself in
our mandatory class. I'm figuring these letters (six
new ones each week) will constitute sufficient proof I'm
"actively seeking employment" to carry me all the way
through to May or June or thereabouts when the funds run
out. If anyone replied to a letter affirmatively (which
would be a shock) I'd simply say no, I've reconsidered,
that particular city's fallen off my "acceptable" list.

It's a scam, sure. Let's face it, for scopers (and
many others) things are not so good these days. Nobody
around here is about to hire a scoper full time. Only
if you have a ten-thousand-dollar home transcription
unit and various fancy modems can you hope to score any
contractual business under the new technological
regime. Soon scopers will be collector's items. This
is doubly true for nightscopers who actually go in to
the office -- we're already almost as rare as authentic
quill-pen-wielding Bartlebyan scriveners.

Tiresome enough? I say again this matter will soon
fade from jyzic description. First, though, the jyzer

will need to be a little more sure the scam will work.

Meanwhile. It's a new life, I mean it really is.
In no way more so than in the dearth of news. No longer
am I informed. Nor will I be. I'm abandoning the news.
Of course I've tried to do this before and failed. Like
quitting pastry or bacon (but especially pastry, and in
particular apple fritters), it's tough. Except it
doesn't seem that way this time. Most days I simply
have no access to current newspapers. It takes a big
effort to go out and buy one -- for the city papers, a
fourteen-mile round trip. And we're too broke to be
doing that anyway.

No doubt this is a bad time to drop out. End of
the liberal era, reactionary attack on the so-called
welfare state, USA spiraling toward new heights of
megalomania overseas and flirting with quasi-fascistic
forms of corporate oligopoly at home. At some point I
may want to start getting more interested in all this,
yes. But not now. Let it run its course for a while.
See if maybe the swarms of bad guys will turn on each
other in their power hunger and mutually self-destruct.
(The wimpy moderates got routed in the election just as
predicted. The nasties now control both houses of
Congress. The hit men. "Contract on USA." I spaced
out mentioning this horror last week.)

*

(Just performed another round of my flushing and
faucet-spinning chores. Saw one of the rascally raccoon
regulars scuttling away on frosty grass from the carport
compost zone. In a move right out of a Hollywood
cartoon the beast nailed me with a chortling little
bandit-eyed backwards glance.)

Rhythms of the new life will take some getting used
to. No real pressures telling me when to sleep, when to
eat, when to JIFT and when to JIRT -- right on down the
line. I'm reinventing myself. (When to shower, when to
shave, when to change clothes, when to offer to help
with this or that, when to get amorous, when to stay out
of harm's way.)

Every other week it's the old life for a day or two

or three. Last week the first snow of the year shut
down grand jury on Wednesday and therefore the new rogue
nightscoper had to go in only one day. That's fine by
me, because Employment Security, until it runs out, will
cover most of what I lose from not being able to work.
     -- And this is Thanksgiving week. Already I'm
gobbling turkey dressing and cranberry sauce (though
peanut butter is my staple these days, along with baked
potatoes and the occasional can of tuna). But the
question is, do we have lots to be thankful for this
year? And I say we might as well admit we do. Don't
know, though, D might soon be turning cantankerous on
me. I'm still trying to nudge her into making a truly
serious effort to find a full-time job. I know she'd
"prefer not to" (that again!) and even if she does find
something she might not be able to stay with it for long
(owing to migraines and/or back flare-ups), but I figure
she should at least be willing to try. Shouldn't she
want her sweet howler to be able to give "Jyzer" his
best shot? Hasn't she gotten her best shot at the
various things she's been aiming at over the past dozen
years and more, closer to fifteen really? If she can't
do it, she can't. But let's find out.
     Thanks but no thanks, she might be saying. Hard to
tell for sure.
     Not that "Jyzer" is going anywhere at the moment.
Might as well come clean: it's just not happening. But
I refuse to start beating myself up about it just yet.
Put it down to delayed fallout from the RIF crisis along
with a dose of unemployment culture shock and various
other new and continuing glooms and megrims. Cut this
Jyzer G right here some much-needed (not that he'd ever
admit it except in these pages) -- slack, yeah.
Slackerman! Give it up for the Slackerman!
     (As on the cold hard floor he finds himself ever
more shifting and squirming. -- But here's a jazz
genius on the radio. Once again he still wants it
straight, no chaser. Also exactly what old contempo G's
still wanting. But then what this jazzman puts on offer
always is just that, no exceptions whatsoever, post-

teen-G lifetime.)

    Tonight we broke down and watched a movie on TV. It was about "Howlers Got No Ballon," as the lady paraphrased the title, using a dance term for leaping ability (which she herself had in abundance before her back went more or less permanently out). Research for "Mentoka Ghosts" as I saw it, this movie. Talk about lightweight stuff. But we laughed anyway, both of us. More than a few times I've played the Cawk bumbler in a hoop hustle of sorts, though never for money. The money part's irrelevant anyway. It's about pecking order. Genderhood. Just like the movie says.

    For three hours this morning thick steam was rising outside the windows almost as if these were Lady V/ Lady S days back in fog city. Sunny and cold after a couple of days of rain will do that.

    What else don't I know? If someone has died or is about to, or is pregnant, just as instances, I'm in the dark. Nobody's telling me anything. Maybe there's nothing to tell. Or maybe I'm being spared across the board because life's already got me in an unbreakable stranglehold. Or maybe a diabolical trick box will fly open, an ES investigation will stumble across Lady S, induce the IRS to take a microscope to old tax returns, get me in heaps of trouble. -- In which case what do we do? If I'm not abandoned first maybe we just head with tails tucked for D's home turf and start over.

    Here I am floundering a long way from any safe port in life. Could I hack living by myself? Probably could scrape up enough part-time scoping jobs to eke out a subsistence urban existence. It would be a scramble for sure. Mostly I'd want to do whatever's necessary to keep plugging away at my life's work. I do know what this work is and that's something. But it's not enough. For the first time just because of being a midlifer I might not be able to land on my feet. -- Merely want to register my awareness of this. Of course I'm not about to give up. Slackerman has his hidden resiliencies.

*

    In glancing back through these pages just now I've

noticed a few loose threads I can tie up. Lots I can't,
but these I can. First, that mysterious ringing phone
at the office on my last night ever as a full-fledged
USAn workforceperson, that wasn't Mother or partner Fran
or brother Rob or any kind of emergency at all, it was D
trying to remind me to pick up a loaf of bread on the
way home. Because I'd be staying home more we'd be
needing more bread and our town store doesn't carry
whole wheat, not even the worst cheapo kind. (And what
about the two-ring signal? She says she used it. I say
she didn't, she spaced it out. In the end we agreed to
disagree without even saying so but nonetheless with
maximally rolling eyes, and I mean all four eyes. As we
seem to be doing more and more these days.)

   -- And now so deeply have I delved into loose
thread No. 1 that No. 2's escaped me.   -- But I do
remember a former U.S. president and former bad
Hollywood actor and world-class reactionary announced
last week he has Alzheimer's disease. Which is
something, just to be able to remember his doing this,
because plenty of my relatives have had Alzheimer's and
someday I probably will too if I get that far, which
itself will take lots of luck; and you always wonder
whether a little advance dose or preview or early onset
might be showing up at any moment, like right now.

   -- Roar of the wall heater all this time. At last
the room is warming up. By and large I take pride in
using the heaters as little as possible. Better to put
on another layer of clothing. I give in only when I can
no longer maintain my grip on the J-stick.   -- Or if
I'm freezing up, head for the utility room and do some
frenzied slammin' and jammin'. (Don't think I've
mentioned this: installation of a new door in the
utility room forced me to move the nerf hoop to a newly
fashioned mini backboard mounted on a mid-room joist
post. And it turns out this new setup beats the old one
hands down. With only my shadow putting up the "D" I
can bust moves to bust all memories of moves busted in
the high-ballon genderhood-proving days of old.)

   The safety net, also a mention for that. I'm now

one of those depending on it, and just when the new
House speaker-to-be and the Christian Knights of the
Far Right want to tear it down. You need help in this
country, you go beg it from charity: this is the new, or
rather renewed, mantra. Get down on your knees and
probably you'll have to kowtow to the sanctioned deity
as well. -- It's a shame, yes, but there's no denying
it jibes with the ascendant spirit of the times. And
these are interesting times. But then they almost
always are if your slant is as it oughta be.

4.

    Turkey-sated. Turkey-drowsy. Sat for a few
minutes with the light off watching flames flicker in
the woodstove. Hot down here. All interior doors open
so as to warm the rest of the house to the extent
possible. Sound of water running upstairs as D readies
herself for bed.
    Some holiday jyze.
    Now she pokes her head in through the foot-square
hole in the wall above the staircase. "Heat hole" we
call it -- positioned there so heat will be drawn up.
Or will rise on its own, like a cold-seeking missile.
(Whatever's right.) -- Reminds me, she does, that a
second lamp hangs on the far side of the loveseat;
having both lamps turned on cuts down on shadows and
contrast. "Turn on your love light." -- But no, I
detected no romantic or erotic subtext, dang it anyway.
    On fingers, dog scent. A daily ritual for us
while Ben and Beryl are away, feeding their critters
and bringing them in for the night. Tonight while
waiting for D in B&B's living room I donned a handy set
of red reindeer antlers (the kind that clip onto your
skull by spring-action device) and snuck up on her.
"They look real on you!" she gasped. Meaning exactly
what I don't know, but I do know what I was reminded

151

of: how truly ursine D herself looked a couple of years
ago when she rose up outside my newly installed shed
window wearing B&B's bearskin rug over her head and
shoulders. One of her best gags ever. To this day the
memory of that big furry befanged snout suddenly
quivering maybe eighteen inches in front of my eyes
turns me "white as a howler" all over again.

A misty night, cool, a few stars peeking through
the ghostly nebular swirls.

The small "pantry" area in which the jyzer at this
moment is languishing: it came into being when the
basement was subdivided for the remodeling last year and
was so dubbed by Mama U. After descending the stairs
from the kitchen you pass through it on the way to the
"library" (straight ahead, also named by her) or the
"utility room" (to the right, Papa U's moniker for it:
he who until recently worked as a chemist for a
utility). The pantry's main feature is a floor-to-
ceiling set of deep built-in shelves running the entire
length of the center wall, with the door to the library
cut through them right in the middle. Currently these
shelves are all jam-packed with still more books, not
the canning and jarring equipment and boxes of bulk
foodstuff and miscellaneous kitchen items Mama U was
projecting for our country-living phase. (And one of
the big questions for the months ahead as we prepare to
move -- as it still appears we'll be doing -- is what
will be the fate of all these books? I mean we want
them! We need them! We love them! Me especially!
-- But I'm guessing we'll have to do without them, or
most of them, for want of shelf space.)

Pause -- I'm advised it would be good to toss
another log on the fire. (Or a batch of books?)

         *   *

An hour later. Turned out to be a lot more than a
log-tossing pause.

While stepping out the new utility-room door to
fetch an armload from the firewood stack I noticed
colored lights flashing faintly in the mist to the
south. At first I thought they were Christmas lights --

someone had picked an apropos time to turn theirs on. I
mean, Thanksgiving dinner's a wrap, what else you got?
What's next? Then leaning out from the veranda
overhang I saw they were cop colors: one set flashing
red, another a stroboscopic blue. Captain Brick's
place, it looked like, third house down.

I told D about all this and we took up positions at
the windows in my study, the best vantage point in the
house. From there we could make out -- barely -- three
cop cars and a fourth vehicle which turned out to be a
large tow truck. Couldn't tell much about what was
going on. Three cop cars means domestic violence, D
said. Brick has a history of same. Jenny is not his
first Filipina Dreamgirl wife; her predecessor was
notoriously wild, used to hang out at the south-county
biker bars, the cops were at Brick's place "almost every
night" (this was before our time; D learned about it at
a water-system meeting). Eventually Brick sent
Dreamgirl No. 1 packing -- back where she came from --
and ordered up a quiet one for No. 2.

I went out to do a little reconnoitering (recalling
a similar incident from Mezzu days, soon to be featured
in "Jyzer"). No whizzing bullets this time as I crept
from tree to tree, but some very impressive female
screams. Was that perhaps the same scream we'd been
hearing on late-summer weekends when we'd thought
someone was being killed at the "ranchette" adjacent to
Brick's place to the east (uphill)? Seemed maybe so.

A male voice barking orders; that was a cop. A
female resisting, screaming, shouting in a Filipino
accent; that was presumably Jenny, although the voice
seemed too big to be hers. (So maybe the former wife
returned to wreak vengeance? Or a friend of Jenny's?
Or a girlfriend of one of Brick's grown biker sons, back
home for an extended-family Thanksgiving repast
featuring after-dinner fun and games?) I was watching
through a grove of pines by the driveway of the next-
door house. Aside from those flashing lights (eerily
beautiful in the mist) I couldn't see much.

Ten or fifteen minutes of that and I stole back

home. Found D still perched in the same position at the
window in my room. Another few minutes and two of the
cop cars left. A few more and the tow truck roared to
life; it backed up the driveway and moments later pulled
out with Brick's ancient green pickup reared on its hind
wheels behind it, seemingly trying to mount it satyr-
like on the move (just the kind of thing you'd expect a
Brick pickup to do). The last of the squad cars
followed, lights flashing.

     Was it a drug bust? A suicide attempt? D
remembered seeing an unusual stack of boxes in Brick's
carport yesterday, the captain himself out checking
them. Grenades for the militia, in which Brick's
supposedly a high honcho? Concealed contraband from
Manila? D'd also seen a strange man in Brick's driveway
at roughly the same time yesterday, a scruffy-looking
bearded howler. And a few hours before that, she said,
someone had knocked at our door while I was asleep, then
driven off in an unfamiliar gray van, leaving no
message. Odd.

     Lots of possibilities here. Strange we heard no
sirens. No more than half an hour earlier we'd been
uneventfully feeding the critters next door. On our way
back I'd suggested a walk around the church loop to burn
off some calories from the Thanksgiving feast, but D
said she was too tired. If we'd taken the walk we'd've
hit Brick's place on the way back at about the same time
the cops did.

     Damn Brick, he's giving mixed-race couples a bad
name around here. On the other hand, he's doing the
same to militias, including the biggest and baddest of
them all (i.e., the U.S. Army -- or would that be the
Marines?). Before much longer anyone in the area
seeking a little peace and quiet may want to move back
to the inner city. (A few weeks ago the grand jury
heard a case involving a gun nut peddling rifles
converted to machine guns a few miles north of here.
Last week a big drug bust -- yet another meth lab hidden
deep in the woods -- went down five miles to the west.)

     It wasn't a murder. The cops would've hung around

a lot longer if it were. And we know somebody's still
home at Brick's place, because shortly after the last
cop left we saw some house lights going off and others
flicking on. But why was the pickup hauled away? Drug-
courier vehicle? Maybe Brick got nailed on an old DUI?

Chances are this will all remain a mystery. The
police-blotter section of the next edition of the south-
county weekly paper might say something about it, but if
not, we'll likely remain in the dark forevermore,
because people around here tend to keep to themselves or
to tight groups (even, usually, at the water-system
meetings, which are annual). The grapevine is a
scraggly shadow of what it must've been in earlier eras.

-- But this is excitement. Certainly it's the
biggest excitement of our time here. It was sheer
serendipity (or misfortune maybe) that I was jyzing away
when it happened.

The ethics of it. The historical and political and
personal tie-ins. Bloody USAn imperial "liberation" of
the Philippines a century ago and colonial control and
neocolonial domination and exploitation of them ever
since, Captain Brick a retired U.S. Army lifer who did
most of his time over there, the poverty, the
hookertowns around U.S. bases -- Dreamgirl entrepreneurs
recruiting in the bars for their catalogs -- my very own
father storming the islands as part of the "I shall
return" operation a generation earlier, the wavy
Filipino sword he "liberated" (that word again!) which
is now standing in shame in a dark corner of my study --
his boss the same corncob-pipe-smoking megalomaniac who
soon became the defacto emperor of Lady U's ancestral
homeland and later the self-proclaimed savior of Lady
S's actual homeland before he was sacked for
insubordination (merely scheming to nuke China).

In a way I've been pondering those ethics and the
larger East/West tie-ins my entire adult life. -- And
therefore no point in pondering them any further in
here, right. Certainly not now anyway.

The two logs I fed into the stove are just about
done for and I'll have to fetch a couple more. Or maybe

just let the fire burn itself out. Nap time coming up.
*

     -- A peaceful holiday, yes, aside from the Brick
incident. I talked to no one but Lady U all day.
Thought a lot about calling ol' Mom but I don't even
know where she is this week. And if I did manage to
track her down I might well be disturbing her. Catching
her at the wrong time can be a painful experience for
both of us these days owing to the mood-altering side
effects of her battery of drugs. And right now I don't
really want to have to be explaining my job situation or
the latest nondevelopments with "Jyzer." But most of
all I fear more bad news about her health. I fear the
deathwatch. Bedside visits, wrangling over the will,
endless medical talk, funeral -- I just want to avoid
all that. There's no denying: I'm in denial. It's
beyond pathetic but I'd just like to stay in it a little
longer. (If things were really, really bad I'd surely
have heard something by now.)
     Ruthlessly suppress that topic. Move on to --
what? Turkey. (Not that Turkey.) Mention that the
first time D roasted a turkey for us she was so
unfamiliar with the bird she cooked it upside down, then
wondered why it seemed almost meatless when she poked it
with a fork to test its readiness. -- But tonight the
two of us working together did just fine. Not only the
bird but the stuffing, rice, potatoes, salad, rolls,
cranberry sauce, pumpkin pie with whipped cream. I'm
still feeling the effects. Damn packed belly keeps
getting in the way as I try to scratch out the week's
jyze in my lap beneath the irritatingly glary twin love
lights.
     To feast like this means we'll have to get by on
scraps next week. But we both figure it's worth it. On
this as on so many things we see eye to eye. After
living enough years with Lady U to hatch a complete
cycle of locusts of the Mentoka/Centropolis variety
(again as of our meeting anniversary last month) I'm
still astounded by this. I no longer would even want to
try to figure out the reasons why it could be.

     -- If worse came to worst, it occurred to me, we
could get by on next to nothing. We could apply for
food stamps. (In fact we qualify right now.) We could
burn wood chopped (illegally) from our wooded wetland
lot for heat and for cooking. We have no rent to pay.
In theory we could come very close to doing without
money. Just the limited scoping income from Jyzer Ink
would be enough to cover the utilities and any
incidental necessities. -- Not that either of us wants
to submit to such a spartan regimen if we can avoid it.
But then again it might be interesting to try -- for a
while. Say a month, two, maybe three months tops.

     I did recall what that other untied-up loose end in
the last entry was. The firm's move. In fact it's
never happened. The lease for potential new digs at a
nearby tower looked unfavorable on closer inspection
and the current landlord offered to let the firm stay
where it is on a month-to-month basis, with a high
probability that the investment outfit from the floor
below won't be needing the space for another year or
two. (I know all this from reading the correspondence
about it on partner Una's desk. I always check to see
what's up -- especially about my own situation. For
weeks nothing new referring to the latter -- the RIF,
I'm talking about -- has been on her desk or partner
Fran's or in the office computer files. I'd been
expecting to come across, for instance, an inquiry from
Employment Security. One could be tucked away in the
hard-copy files, which I haven't peeked at recently, but
otherwise I've found nothing. -- And no, most likely
they're not aware I try to keep tabs on all this. I
reckon they're oblivious more or less by choice; they
simply don't want to be thinking about such a sorry
matter any more than they have to.)

     As it happened I ran into reporter Naomi Monday
night when I went in to do her grand-jury finals. She
had a job scheduled for the next day, she said, and she
wanted me to do the scoping on it even though it wasn't
grand-jury or government work, strictly speaking. If
the partners objected, she said, she would take the

heat. I said fine and went in Tuesday night to do it
and then again last night to punch in the corrections
and print the finals (because the bound transcript must
go out tomorrow morning). That's a lot of traveling for
a 111-page job, especially since three-quarters of Jyzer
Ink's $88.80 charge for it will be deducted from my
Employment Security check. So I prefer to look at it
as a kind of investment designed to mature shortly
after the ES benefits run out. Jyzer Ink is showing it
can get the job done, even on a holiday expedite order,
and at no extra charge.

(Or to put the financial aspect of it differently,
I was working for $5.54 an hour, which is 64 cents above
the state minimum wage. Or factoring in the two days'
commuting time of approximately nine hours, $1.77 an
hour. And the commute itself costs $13.60.)

Naomi also said she was plenty upset with reporter
Verna for backing out on our agreement. Neither of us
can figure out why she did it. "There's got to be more
going on with her," Naomi noted, "than meets the eye."
May have to do with a messy divorce Verna reportedly
(office gossip) went through a decade ago -- domestic
violence, cops, bankruptcy, bad checks written by the
vengeful ex. Naomi asked whether Jyzer Ink would still
be able to do her scoping if Verna were out of the
picture for good; and I said it probably would but "the
board of directors" (wink wink) would be reviewing the
entire setup at year's end. Had to handle it that way
-- can't let Naomi think I'm too easy or too desperate.

Meanwhile poverty keeps nipping at us. Last week
the newspaper delivery people (for the city daily) took
back their kitschy plastic roadside box. Two weeks from
now we'll have to stop using D's old car when its
insurance expires. That means I'll lose the option of
driving to the home port and parking there overnight
when I go into the city, because D will need to have
functioning wheels here in case some health emergency --
or any kind of emergency -- arises when I'm away.

One surprising note. Apparently because I'm
keyboarding so much less my wrists ache afterwards when

                    [Blank Jyze]

I do any at all. My eyes also hurt afterwards and even
more during. At odd times -- usually when I'm in bed --
the keyboard calluses (left hand especially) seem almost
to be vibrating, as if they miss the usual pounding,
sort of like sports muscles spasming after the season's
over. And with or without the vibrations, sleeping is
harder during the day and not sleeping harder at night.
     In short, use it or lose it. And I'm losing it in
a number of ways. The protective adaptations of the
wily old nightscoper are fading fast.

                    CHAPTER NINE

          [Theory of a Unified Jyzefield]

                         1.

     Came crunching up. Shedward. It's again so cold
in here the J-stick (still trusty No. 5) keeps sliding
out of my fingers. The heater's not doing it for me yet
nor is the extra layer of sweats.
     -- But here's the noisily insistent Ripper the
half-grown cat, now tucked inside my zip sweatshirt,
just her mug sticking out where the zipper splits at my
chest. And what a mug: black fur tinged with shades of
gold and brown ("calico"), bright green eyes, long
whiskers like a crayfish. Now sanding down my left
thumb with her tongue. Purring loudly enough, or
almost, to drown out the heater's grind.
     All week it's been weather. If it's not a storm
it's a storm warning. Advisory this, Arctic Express
that. Then this morning Winter Wonderland, sun and
bright blue skies and close to a foot of new snow on the
ground. "Snow falling on alders." And then falling off

alders, all day long, loudly, as if the world around us
were in the early stages of a slow collapse.

I was almost trapped in the city -- might have
stayed there today except D's car was parked on the
street by the courthouse above the foot-ferry dock. The
town cops could've hauled it away, which would've been
fine by itself since it becomes uninsured as of next
week (and is almost twenty years old), but then we'd've
been hit, by mail, with a huge bill.

(Here's Ripper's left paw pumping away; I can just
barely feel the claws pricking my chest through the
layered henleys. Except for the one paw sticking out
she's now completely curled inside the sweatshirt.)

Some drive home it was. Scary, super-cautious,
exhilarating. Everywhere cars spinning, gliding
sideways, sliding into ditches. A convoy rolling slowly
along the freeway -- the bendy and hilly county highway
was too risky -- behind a huge snowplow kicking up a
white plume ten or twelve feet high like a massive bow
wave. Or could say the trailing cars, each with its own
lesser snow plume, resembled a row of waggly duckling
tailfeathers imitating big mama duck's up ahead. And
treacherous ice patches booby-trapping the side roads.

But that was then and this is: midnight. After the
storm is the cold and the silence. Scarcely a leaf left
on the bigleaf maple out there or any other tree owing
to the boisterous winds of the past few weeks. But all
branches are frosted, two-toned, heavily weighed down
with tall snow slices except where the slice has already
slipped off. (A few scattered leaves clinging to the
bush to the far left looking like powder puffs or maybe
furry-faced otter pups.) (And the Jyzer Ink business
license, I might note, is still posted in its
"conspicuous" spot straight ahead, unseen by anyone
since its last mention in these pages except maybe a few
curious deer, and then only the boilerplate back side.)

-- Thinking last night how marvelous things are
right now, if only I could feel it. Or feel it more.
Because the uncertainty is too great. But otherwise I
tick off the attributes of this current life and find it

just about ideal. With only one exception, everything's
working out as hoped. You just don't get to have the
euphoria along with it, that's all.

The good news came in waves. A card from Mother.
D's tampons back in use. A check from ES.

(I'm warm on the front side but cold on the back.
And Ripper is squirming. In hunching over to
accommodate the beast I'm straining my back, much like
an expectant mother. If I may presume, that is. And
why not? "Empathic imaginative projection" -- jyze to
be sure firmly favoring frequent flourishes of same --
and if you frown on alliterative flare-ups, F you!)

Of course Mother will die anyway. How soon, how
horribly, no way to know. Yet she flew home from the
winter house so she and Jim Q. could see a therapist of
some sort who's treating his bipolar disease (if that's
what it is; they're not sure) and also counseling their
relationship. And they had to wheel her off the plane.

Oh the ambivalence. The wish to be closer but also
the fear. And the fact of so many differences. And
sister Barb being there and acting so piously
proprietary about it all. And Lady U being in many ways
beyond Mother's comprehension and what's more not so
good herself at comprehending across such a large gap.
It's not even all that unusual a story. "Except in the
details." (But contrary to rumor the devil is not there
-- or at least not the devil that worries me most. That
one's in the macro, mercilessly flinging out the awful
unintended and/or ignored consequences of the economy of
capital bigness.) (So take that, Mr. D.)

Meanwhile I've decided -- the one exception noted
above, as if it weren't obvious -- to put "Jyzer" on
hold and focus for the time being on gearing up for its
successors. A serious move. Strangely enough (but no),
this move seems to have stirred up some renewed interest
in "Jyzer" itself. This I'm trying to ignore until it
reaches critical mass. And in the hope of inducing such
a reach as soon as possible, I'm also about to begin
typing up this past spring and early summer's J-book,
the first full volume. The idea is to nudge myself by a

kind of osmosis (or call it a trick of perspective) into
the excited frame of mind I was in back then.

   Maybe it'll work and maybe it won't. But I have to
try something new. I've been spinning my wheels way too
long on this.

   "In Search of Lost 'Jyzer.'" Not even wearing the
cornball "DREAM" cap all day for two days straight could
help me locate it.

   (Black nose poking out. Stretching leg and paw. A
few feline squawks and again a full-leg retraction.)

   -- Several days into December now. For me a whole
different mindset locks into place as we enter the year-
end borderlands. And the right sort of things have been
happening to confirm that the crossing itself looms
ahead. A big box of gift-wrapped packages arrived from
the U's. And just this morning at the public market in
the city (all a-bustle with seasonal trade, the outdoor
merchants massively bundled up against the cold) I
scored my first batch of free newsstand calendars. From
the looks of the new edition next year will surely be
terrific. (And because the coming year almost always
looks that way on these calendars, and because they're
greeting-card size, I usually slip one in with most of
my Christmas cards and plan to do so again this year.)

   The scope office is still there. Not too many
changes except the holiday decorations are up, such as
they are. The world of the downsized firm. Leftovers
from dayscoper Thomas's farewell party, which was held
at lunch hour Wednesday and of course I missed it (and
his lockbox on the shelf above mine is now unlocked and
empty, even the embossed red name-tape gone). Also an
invite on the bulletin board for this year's Christmas
party on Friday the 15th at noon, but it's not meant for
me and I wouldn't go if it were. Haven't attended one
in years. And back then went just as a matter of form,
and only if they had the party in the evening so I could
stay on to do my scoping after everyone left.

   But this jyzebyte. On the secretary's desk was the
annual notice of tax rates from Employment Security.
And I was delighted to discover that the checks I'm

receiving won't affect the firm's rate until next year,
that is, the year after the one that begins next month.
The partners apparently won't even know I'm on the dole
until a full year from now when they get the next annual
notice. And so: this too is part of the good-news wave.
Unless it's concealing something I'm not aware of yet.
(And surely it is -- but maybe it's not that bad.)

And this: I'm now finally in full compliance with
the Employment Security rule that a benefits recipient
be "actively seeking work." I mailed out another batch
of letters containing resumes -- sent them to a dozen
reporting firms in a dozen different cities from coast
to coast, in each case saying I might be moving to that
city at some unspecified point in the "near future"
("near" by what time scale the letter didn't say) and
was looking for full-time scoping work and if they
expected such to become available "soon" (same caveat)
would they please let me know how to apply for a job.
who knows, I might even get a nibble or two. But if so
I'm not required to respond -- and as mentioned before,
I'd almost certainly start having second thoughts about
moving to that particular city. And I get to do that;
the regulations say so. They can't force me to move to
another state, or to move at all, to take a job.

Or maybe I'm not fully understanding the regs. But
I think I am. And this is the course I intend to follow
unless it's challenged. Each week six more letters (the
regs say only three "job-seeking efforts" are required
per week but I'm playing it safe). This week's batch
will go to firms in six different states, all but one
more than two thousand miles from here. The names of
the firms, addresses and whatnot, come from the official
national court-reporter sourcebook. And I print out the
letters and resumes on the office system -- keep the
templates for them stored on a diskette in my lockbox.
And bring home an extra copy of each letter in case ES
comes pounding on the door demanding proof of my claims.

It's a good racket so far. Legit too. "By the
book." When it eventually plays out (hopefully not
until next summer) I'm planning to keep scoping part-

time for reporter Naomi just as I'm doing now under the
Jyzer Ink license (which I'll be renewing this week for a
full year) and otherwise to devote all my time to the
real work. This will depend, however -- alas -- on D's
finding a job somewhere along the way, preferably fairly
soon. -- But no point in worrying about that right now.

(Having this business license, by the way, hasn't
made me immortal or turned me into a fictitious person.
That's only for corporations. Jyzer Ink being a mere
sole proprietorship, I'm it and it's me; its life span is
limited to my own. Can't call myself a corporado after
all. Sole prop.'s the one.)

(Ripper's head hanging out where the zipper splits
-- lolling upside down like an otter aswim on its back,
all whiskery-faced. This is just too goddamned cute for
words. I otter be ashamed, har har. Belly up to the bar
at The Ott Spott, nyuk nyuk. -- All this Mezzu nonsense
perpetrated in pursuit of the old jyze spirit, that's my
excuse.)

-- Nor do I want it to be thought I'm romanticizing
poverty. No way! As yet we're not quite poor enough to
be really poor. True poverty is only lurking nearby.
Even so my crass jokes about it are direct-wired to an
undercurrent of fear. Most likely I wouldn't be joking
at all if true poverty hit. (At this point we still
haven't applied for food stamps.) -- D jokes too. Got
off a good one today -- I've already used a version of it
myself in these pages, but without her operatic chops and
stage veteran's timing -- about burning my manuscripts
for heat "like they do in 'La Boheme.'"

-- About the big incident with the cops at Captain
Brick's place, no new word. The very next day we saw
Brick out tooling around with Jenny in the same green
Ford pickup that was hauled away the night before; both
cheerily waved. Nothing in the south-county paper this
week. Nothing from the rumor mills. (This green pickup,
I'll note, is a more or less exact duplicate of the one
Brick totaled in August, the gaunt twisted skeleton of
which now rides a set of cinderblocks in his backyard as
he cannibalizes it for parts. Back then jyze was too

preoccupied elsewhere to take proper notice of this
major neighborhood event.   -- But who would've believed
two such vintage pickups could still exist on the same
continent, much less in our tiny backwoods burg?   -- Or
maybe even three, if we were wrong and the cops still
have the second one.)

Brrr. Jyze has gone on too long: into a second
extra page now. Probably I shouldn't try another
session out here on such a cold night. (Did finish a
reread of those marvelous medieval essays on idleness
Japanese style. Did decide to rely exclusively on the
Mentoka papers for news of the world, thus ensuring I'll
get everything about a week late -- which does make
skimming the papers a whole lot easier.) (No essays on
idleness, by the way, no zuihitsu; and no zuihitsu, no
jyze. Simple fact. -- But also no chronbook, no
journal; no journal, no J-book; no J-book, no J-ize (the
verb); no J-ize, no jyze. So peck on that you jyngine
beauties! -- And no Mentoka shift, no jyze either;
wouldn't want to leave that out.)

Ripper will not like this but it's time to go.
(Her stubbly chin now resting on my left wrist -- she's
half emerged from the sweatshirt, like an adolescent
kangaroo awkwardly climbing out of the pouch.) And
little cat hairs shedding all over these pages and
jamming up the nib. Ach, stop! Unhand that beast!

2.

True jyze this time. Or an attempt. Another.
Once again. Or it simply will be as it will.
-- Straining lower back muscles because I'm back on
the cushions in J. central. "Back where a pain is a
pain." Or yeah, where jyze began.
And now it can open out from itself in new ways.
Whyzat? Because "Jyzer"'s been banished to the shed for
the duration. It's been iced. Cold storage. It won't

be allowed back in the house until it gets its act
together. (And this the very week I was planning --
back in August -- to finish up the rough.)

Admittedly I'm wondering whether it's true, as Mama
U purportedly said on the phone tonight -- "and without
a trace of sarcasm," according to D -- that I'm "sweet
and good-natured." Certainly I'd like to think so. Not
always but at least occasionally -- or maybe better to
say just in certain dark corners hidden away down deep?
And doesn't even this minimal claim conflict with the
dyspeptic jyzer tone? (And all the rhetorical self-
interrogation with its many question marks?)

Fire away. Go ahead and whip up a full crock of
jyzey nonsense and don't fret about it.

Being as it's the time of year it is I expect even
these uncommercial jazz folks on the radio to pump out a
few Christmas tunes and usually they oblige, like it or
not. (Of course public radio will be one of the first
targets of the fire-breathing dog-eat-doggers now
swarming into the national capital. Just hope it all
backfire-breathes on them, like a torchy version of
pissing into the wind. Chances it will? Not bad.
These people have no answers. What they think are
answers are the very policies which produced the crisis
in the first place starting roughly a century ago.)
(Crisis? Is there anything that isn't? Or for the
likes of a Cawk raised in the USA burbs anything that
truly is? -- But we'll soon be getting a new personal
as well as national take on all this, I'd wager.)

Almost time for another unemployment check to roll
in. No botheration from them so far. How long can this
last? Months maybe. (Just a little I'm embarrassed to
mail off the claim -- don't want to do it from our local
post office. But then do so anyway just to show I can
still be a tough guy if I want to be. Or need to be
maybe, as now. -- And how pitiful this is.)

More reclusion. These days I'm speaking with
almost no one except D. Why should I? I'm supposed to
be suffering. What's more I'm also supposed to be in a
reclusive creative funk. And indeed I am in just that.

[Theory of a Unified Jyzefield]

All day every day as much as I can bear. Right now it's
delicious. Other moments it grinds painfully (but
mesmerically even so, at least for me).

     Trouble is, most of the deliciousness has to do
with the jyze manifesto. Yes, typing up the slender
first volume of these scratchings ("Jyzeburst") has got
me back into puzzling about that. Jyze, it seems, has
ten "arms," something like a doubly mutant octopus: this
I've discovered. Over the past week I've churned out
several thousand words about these arms and other
anatomical features. Which is not to say the manifesto
("Tractatus Jyzicus"?) is going anywhere. It's just
what's happening now while the mills are grinding away
down deep. "The healing process." Just a way I can say
I'm doing something, as with typing up these "Burst"
pangs. And I know it, yeah. (Oops -- I meant to write
"pages," not "pangs." But now I can't bear to strike
"pangs." Because now it's birthed. Spank its bottom!)

     Of course it's ironic that all of a sudden jyze of
the real-time variety (JIRT) is pretty much all I've got
going. Back in May the only way I was able to talk
myself into starting up what I'm now calling "Jyzeburst"
was by abjuring that specific possibility. Above all I
would never type it up. Period. Flat-out.

     One difference though. At times in the past,
including briefly last July, I've abandoned all jyze and
jyzelike activities -- meaning urjyze and protojyze --
for the duration while fictifying. This time I intend
to keep the JIRT jyze going, and not just for the rest
of this volume, but permanently, no matter what else I
may be working on. And I have a strong hunch I can do
it. Because this time I have vagueness to retreat into.
It's a sanctioned option. May not seem like much but
it's crucial: it's the escape hatch, it's the space
where I can't be reached by anyone or anything. It's
the doubly mutant jyzopus vanishing into its own cloud
of permanent black ink. Or just call it dark territory.

     (I did ask the old "Jyze Rules" ruler if "Jyzer"
should be banished. It said yes, on the first throw
and then two out of three and then four out of seven

(or six actually; the seventh wasn't needed).)
        -- Old partner Fran, in this season of conspicuous
charity she's suddenly feeling so bad about her wicked
deeds that she sent me a Christmas card with a patchwork
teddy bear on the front. Her two-sentence note inside
laments that we never get a "chance" to see each other
anymore so I should ring her up for a chat some night.
A little RIF-rap maybe? Wotta hoot. I should do it out
of sheer perversity. Or to keep her off balance.
"Franny & Zuihitsu." (If she cares so much shouldn't
she at least have inquired about my progress in finding
a new job? Asked if she could do anything to help?)
        It's our only Christmas card so far, except for the
one from E.Z., the auto dealer who sold us our wagon.
But this lack is nothing new or unexpected. And it's
still early, at least by our standards. (If even a tiny
hint of special pleading seems to be surfacing here, I
sternly remind myself, STOMP IT OUT.)
        -- And what? Typing up the opening entries of
"Burst," I meant to say, has been slow going because old
No. 3's raggedy slashes and blots and bleed-throughs,
though visually arresting at times, too often make the
text damnably hard to decipher. How much easier it was
when the content was freshly in mind! But things are
speeding up now as I move into the pages following the
changeover to J-sticks No. 4 and 5.
        Stretch. Writing in this posture is what was doing
in my back last summer. But I can't just give it up.
I'd like to have a writing table down here, yes, if only
I had some say on such matters. Best, though, not to
rile anyone up. On the phone tonight, D told me, Mama U
asked if we'd begun packing yet. And not so jokingly
either. (How surprised they'd be if I rebelled against
all this. I've been so pliable for so long they can't
imagine me any other way. And this no doubt is what
Mama U was really referring to with her alleged "sweet
and good-natured" remark. And well she should! But
mainly I want to be able to carry on with the writing.
For now I continue to think it's best to keep the clamps
on myself -- persist in looking at this as a matter of

being in it for the long haul. Go along to get along.
Of course once again it's true if I had independent
bargaining power things would be instantly different.
However, I'll go on grooving on powerlessness. It's
something else. And I'm learning a lot, yes I am.)

        -- By the way, it finally happened. Every day I
get up at three-fifty so as to be ready to take a call
from the office between four and five. "Just in case."
Last week, surprisingly, one came in: dayscoper Doris
informing me that reporter Naomi was covering reporter
Verna's grand jury for the week and wanted me to scope
it. (And after imparting this, old Turkey finally broke
through to the personal for the first time since the RIF
crisis began: "So...how ya doin'?" she inquired. The
soul of cheeky compassion. "I'm hangin' in there," I
said. That's it. Don't want to alienate her too much
but neither will I stoop to pretending to be buddy-buddy
anymore, or at least not if I can help it. In truth I'd
like to kick her ass from here to scoper limbo and back
-- or forget the "back"; leave her hanging right there
slowly twisting. -- But wait, scoper limbo is where I'm
already hanging myself slowly twisting! -- In any case
I sure hope she's not being worked to the bone now
without me there to cover for her as I so selflessly did
so often over the years.) (Okay, just this one last
bile release now complete and I'm purged for good.)

        And because of the unexpected scoping work and a
decision to reduce the portion of my earnings I report
to ES (assigning a larger chunk to tax-deductible
expenses for Jyzer Ink: depreciation, transportation,
work clothes, reference books, etc.) I'm now a couple of
hundred bucks better off than I thought I'd be at this
point. Or will be when the next ES check arrives. And
am I prudently planning to set aside this windfall for a
rainy day (of which the near future will surely bring an
abundance)? Hell no! Instead I'll be going wild for
Christmas. An anti-Scroogeian minibinge for me and D.
Also six more months of the Wachute daily. And soon
subscribing to a new Mentoka weekly to help with
preparations for "Mentoka Dreams," which I've scheduled

myself to start churning out next spring. (Will it happen? "Jyzer" must come first. Admittedly things are getting a little tight with the whole damn trilogy.)

    -- At the office I found a new employee roster posted by the receptionist's workstation. No longer was I listed under "Staff"; now I was under "Other." In revenge I helped myself to two dozen designer apples. Every year a huge box of these apples arrives by UPS in early December, I know not why or from whom. Before now I've never dared to grab more than a few. This time I packed such a heavy load I was staggering under it by the time I reached the ferry. And the next day I made off with a dozen more. If the office staff doesn't like it I guess they'll just have to take down the "Have at 'em" sign taped on the wall above the box.

    Yeah. I'm showing them all right. They'll be sorry one of these days.

    Meanwhile I've lost the snap-on hood for my winter coat. Looked everywhere for it. A commute like mine demands a rainproof hood. This means I'll have to go back to wearing my fall jacket (whose hood is built in) with an extra layer or two of heavy henleys underneath. It also means D won't be exclaiming anymore when she picks me up at the dock, "Ooh, you look so sexy in your black coat! Let's hurry home so we can hoss around!" (All right, I'll admit this happened only once and it was at least three years ago. Maybe this highlight is getting a little too grainy to stay on the reel.)

    -- Did jyze lead anywhere this time? Nope. Am I surprised? Am not. The real stuff often won't. Better not to force it. Not always maybe but a jyzer does need those pressure-free entries. Just to drift. "Jyzopus adrift in the longeur deeps." Whether a reader will catch the jyzer's drift, or want to, and especially when the prime focus is fictive -- well, who knows. And who's clamoring to know? If anyone is, let your inquiries be heard! And if not, fine. How it is.

    This week I'll be trying to squeeze in a lot of typing at the office. I've decided I'm not stopping with the first volume; I'm going for broke. If lucky,

by this time next week I'll have in hand a hard-copy
rough draft of the whole of "Burst" right up to the
present, or at least most of it. -- And I do mean
rough. I do I do I do.
     Excellent, I'm done. Can go curl up beneath my old
coats and sweatshirts. Listen for that infamous hum in
the night. (It could be coming from the transformers on
the high-power lines just outside. Though I'll grant
that wouldn't explain why people claim to be hearing it
in many other areas -- from sea to humming sea.)

                              3.

     Try again. Go for just barely short of incoherent.
A goal much harder to reach than it sounds, or at least
if the reaching is intentional.
     "Back where." On the post office's biggest day of
the whole goddamn year, so we can all be proud. And we,
D and I, went there, our town post office, even
quarreled a bit about the exact timing of the visit.
The window closes for an hour at noon. Before or after,
which will it be? Have it your way! No, have it yours!
Jeez!
     Quarrels are popping out all over. I've made it
plainly known I'm hoping for up to eighteen months of
financial help from her, D, in which she'll more or less
match what I put in. Now she's gone off on a teenager-
like "life sucks" kick, and I don't think the timing is
coincidental. About all she can say for us these days
is we're the only ones who would put up with each other.
This does not bode well for our future well-being. But
maybe we'll find a way to muddle through. The fact
that we always have before ought to count for something.
     Rain. Lots and lots and lots of rain this week.
Rain right now. Dripping and tapping and splattering
outside. Xylophone music playing in here or maybe it's
vibraphone. Whatever it is, it adds a sprightly

counterpoint to the rain's ordinary old plinkety-plank.

The biggest shocker, it's still got me reeling: it appears sister Barb's gone religious. Under cover of a preachy photocopied group Christmas letter to her brothers, mother, and Jim Q., she sent out copies of a sermon delivered by a cranky big-time theologian of half a century ago. My packet just came in today. I'm so taken aback I haven't been able to decide yet whether I should be insulted. Probably I should, but should I run with it? (Are you running with me, Jyze-us?)

Mother's back at the winter house now. Another card came in from her. She's in lots of pain. Says she'll be undergoing tests and will know more on the 27th. Also says Barb has a new "beau," a coworker in the same office it appears, and they'll be touring Portugal together for a month starting in early January. Is he perhaps behind Barb's conversion? (I must say religion is probably where she should've been all along. All that moral certainty about whatever ideas or principles she was espousing at the time, no matter how wildly they conflicted with the previous month or year's notions, not to mention others of the current array. I just shake my head. Nana's influence, I guess, from all those visits up to Lahontan. Also the Fritsch Teutonic stiffness and properness inherited from Gram's side. The exalting of mysticality and tradition no matter how superstitious and antiquated and pernicious. The condescension. Oy, I dread having to deal with this.)

-- Well, maybe it's not as bad as it looks. Best not to jump to conclusions. And I suppose it wouldn't hurt to recall that my own heritage is much like Barb's and I too visited Lahontan many times -- probably more. In fact, unlike her, I was born there.

"Twas the week before Christmas." My Christmas shopping for this year is mostly done. Books and a new round of personalized hummingbirds for all, including D (who also will be getting a jyze present, assuming we're still on speaking terms). Only one person outside our two families is on the list: reporter Naomi (for her a couple of T-shirts Mama U embroidered and kindly sent to

us to pass along as gifts to whomever). I also came up
with a boxful of altered cards using a new "stampling"
technique, rubber-stamping semi-randomly atop already
existing cards from last year's half-price table -- all
showing a motley caravan of camels plodding along in
the desert with city minarets shimmering in the
background. And I like the way they came out.

*

(The heater just flipped off on its own as I was
standing up to turn it off. Serendipity! -- Don't need
a whole lot of heat considering it's in the mid-fifties
out there at midnight.)

Meanwhile all else is going along. No new
glitches. Also no new triumphs or breakthroughs or
anything remotely approaching same on the JIFT. All I
can say is "Jyzer" is still locked up in the shed and
"Burst" is typed up through the end of October. In the
next few days I'll be taking the "Burst" thing right up
to the foaming edge (which would be the sentence going
down right now if I started typing this instant and
didn't stop until I ran out of jyze). Therefore an
alternative title presents itself for inspection and
immediate rejection: "Tale of a Self-Begetting JIRTel."

Knees spread wide, pressing up close against the
wooden stand. Cushions. This has got to be one of the
worst possible postures for writing no matter of what
kind and somehow I keep winding up in it.

And a bellyful of rice. And one of those designer
apples right here, it's far too perfect to eat but I
must chomp into it regardless. Sin. Pile it on. "Sin
becomes you." (A phrase whose meaning seems to flick
back and forth, from diabolical to sacerdotal, could
say, sort of like an ethical version of a certain crazed
philosopher's favorite rabbit/duck optical illusion.)

I've got about half a dozen books I'm reading
simultaneously. This is one of the advantages of having
all or nearly all one's time free for one's own work.
Nor do I think I'm using this reading as a way to avoid
writing. True, I'm not writing anything at the moment
(except this), but the avoidance is for other reasons

173

[Jyzeburst]

(the Christmas stuff, for one thing, along with a
heavier-than-expected scoping workweek, but mainly
because my spirit's just not right for grappling with
anything that demands sustained concentration).

     Tomorrow I go in again to do almost four hundred
pages of finals. After that, barring the unexpected, no
more scoping work until the second week in January
(because grand jury takes the holidays off and the feds
rarely slate depositions then). During this period I'm
aiming to get the "Mentoka Dreams" outline ready to go.

     -- Hoo boy I'm tired tonight. Slept only three
hours this afternoon. As usual in the current era my
schedule got all bollixed up over the weekend. So far
I'm not making a big effort to come up with a new sleep
pattern more suitable for the new circumstances. After
all these years living by Nightscoper Upside-down Time
(NUT, still) I don't know if I could do it if I tried.
Would it make any real difference? Probably not.

     Digging back in search of the original enerjyzers.
Excavate that hurt. Let's see. Poke at the sore spots.
Rub conflicts together. Stick a finger in it. How
about stirring up some guilt? Should I merely suppress
most of my abundant ambivalence? Move on too soon? Can
I do better at holding everything steady while exploring
the tensions (like sliding in and out of the strings of
a harp without being shredded)?

     -- D's venerable car, by the way, has been put out
to pasture, literally almost, in a weedy patch at the
head of the driveway, its insurance expired and its
registration about to be. Already it's slowly sinking
into the mud, sort of like the skull of a very large
metallic steer disappearing into shifting desert sands.
Now I'll start using the wagon, which in the nearly two
years we've had it I've driven exactly once, from the
county bus stop to the house, about two miles tops. But
I won't drive it much. Better it should be here in case
D needs it when I'm in the city. I'll take the bus when
one's available; when one's not (on weekends mostly) D
will drop me off and/or pick me up at the foot ferry.
Or if she lines up a job (am I dreaming?) with weekend

174

hours, we'll have to come up with some other solution.
Maybe break out one more time my old broken-pedaled
bicycle (and hope for iceless midwinter roads).

*   *

Jumped around some on the nerf court while jyze
central was heating up. Before that read a batch of new
haiku translations as I downed peanut-butter sandwiches
and on the other side of the glass the rain fell.
Rivers everywhere rapidly on the rise says the radio.

"Taking No. 5 out for a jyze." -- Are you running
with me, brand X? A slo-mo dash for the scratch patch
(natch).

Still blinking about Barb's latest spiritual
makeover. And at the rocky-road mix of piety and subtle
little digs in her group cover letter. But far be it
from me to mock or disparage. On the contrary: I'm
proud to have a sister contributing to the reenchantment
of the world. (Ha. I'd like some reenchantment to
happen, yeah, but it better not be under the aegis of
the same old deities who got us into the mess we're in
now, and especially not the one she's currently
cottoning up to, the single most culpable of them all.)

At any moment we'll be rolling across the solstice.
The paper says sunset would be at four-twenty today were
there even the slightest prospect of our seeing it
(above the clouds one could always see it, of course,
but up that high I'd think it would come at a
significantly different time).

Vagueness and emptiness. My life is not really
like this. It's one excitement after another and that's
the truth, with only here and there a disappointment
mixed in. I chime better with the zest and gusto of the
haiku master I've been reading lately than with, say,
the anxiety and anomie of Barb's Cold War theologian.
Most of the time I have to work hard to tease out these
latter emotions from my inner tangle. Granted the past
few months have been a rather prominent exception.

-- Pondering, well, am I ruining the jyze concept
by opting to type it up and thus, in essence, take it
public? (Getting it all the way there would be

175

something else again.) Truly it does seem harder to let
myself just ride the current right now. (Radio news
break: another weapon incident at the White House. The
third in two months, this time a homeless man shot to
death while making a run at the Rose Garden fence with a
pocketknife. Apparently. Details still sketchy.)

The white floor-to-ceiling curtain is closed. At
the bottom in the one-inch gap between curtain and
carpet an edge of light cut in the same wavy shape as
the curtain's folds undulates faintly like a ghost snake
slowly slithering in place. If I were to open this
curtain, a redwood bench would appear. The town manager
could sit there if he happened by and wanted to narrate
our little domestic drama Grover's Corners style for a
few minutes before moving on to do the same at all the
other houses. The bench looks out on birds, cats, high
grass, a big leafless apple tree, a small leafless apple
tree, a wall of deliquescent woodland greenery streaked
vertically with the inky near black of tree trunks.

Here's a jazzy assertion that Santa Claus is coming
to town. How tame and predictable this kind of jazz now
seems -- certainly nothing outrageous about it -- yet
it's still a big step outside the saccharine pop realm
and plenty pleasurable for me.

Huh? I've now lived up to my lowest jyze
expectations. I've made it to the sign of the three
invisible stars. Again. The streak is intact. Now can
go bolster my spirits with more haiku. Or maybe it'll
be nikki bungaku, a Japanese literary diary of sorts, in
this case written by a different, perhaps kinder and
gentler, Lady U (well, as seen from a millennium's
distance anyway). "Skazmo saijiki." I like it!

4.

A toast to Christmas. From a glass of authentic
bootleg hooch called Ol' Grizzlie Bite. The bottle with

its hilarious hand-drawn label, eccentric spelling and all, standing right behind the glass with the crackling cubes. Nasty stuff too. And I need it. But nowhere near as much as I was afraid I would.

So what's the deal here? "Jyze After Hours" -- one in the morning or so. -- And now from 1925 comes "Sandy Closs Blues," as the DJ calls it. As a Sandy myself I know I'll like this. (And do.)

The good news is Mother's still alive and kicking. That's the bad news too, of course, no denying, she says so herself. But for most of our two hours plus on the phone she sounded great.

Mother even helped us, though inadvertently, ease out of an embarrassing little jam. Ben and Beryl and the kid (two-year-old) dropped by bearing gifts when we failed to show up for their Christmas Eve party. We all stood around the kitchen making awkward nice. The gifts were to thank us for watching the critters while they were away. Included was this bottle of moonshine whiskey made by an acquaintance of the truly backwoods friends they were visiting in the far northeast corner of the state (the choice of poisons also alluding to the incident, mentioned earlier -- and now apparently infamous statewide, in a sense -- involving me, D, the shed, and B&B's bear rug: "We saw that bottle and we both said, 'Dani and Glen!'"). -- After a wincingly cringeful twenty minutes or so the phone rang, thank god. Mom. That we were waiting for the traditional Christmas Eve call from her had been our excuse for not showing up at the party in the first place.

Not that they're bad people, B&B. They're fine. Excellent. We're the unsociable weirdos, the isolatos.

And now into the deep of the night with one ear cocked for the sound of rooftop hooves (usually it's cats and once in a while raccoons going at it up there atop the veranda but tonight under the spell of Ol' Grizzlie Bite -- talk about steel teeth! -- who knows what I might detect).

Nostalgia. Relief. Corniness. It seems this night is still the best of them all for me. Warmest.

Most hopeful. Most spirited. Most merrily awash in
memories. As I told ol' Mom, I sure did luck out to
have a childhood that left me thinking of Christmas this
way.

For poor D it's not the same. She doesn't mince
words: "I hate Christmas. I always did." Merry and
bright these days she's not. I can tell because of the
frequency with which I find myself making excuses for
her. Not to others, or not usually. To myself. It's
just surprising she hasn't been this way more often over
the long haul (but the frequency may be changing now).
Congenital bad health and nasty injuries created this
streak in her, forcing her to give up the two pursuits
she's ever really cared about and in both cases just as
her career was taking off, the two a decade apart:
diving and dance. That's my theory anyway. Not that
she's ever complained about any of it.

Rice and bell pepper beef, our Christmas dinner.

But I'm happy regardless. Why? In addition to
anything already cited? That is, how dare I? Because I
just read over the typed draft of "Jyzeburst" -- which D
will be receiving as a slightly delayed Christmas
present (delayed because hers for me, she revealed
tonight, also isn't quite ready yet) -- and I think it's
not so bad. And right now, at least, that's saying a
lot, especially compared to what I'd have no choice but
to say about anything else I've been working on lately.
-- Comes to 140 pages so far in the usual single-space
boxed transcript format, "Burst" does, which is just
about exactly one typed page for every two handwritten
pages; and I'll be adding the pages from the last two
entries, this one and the one now planned for New Year's
Eve, and making a jazzy/jyzey/bursty cover for it with
the rubber stamps and J-stick No. 3's splashy
scratchings and then binding the whole thing on the
machine at the office. And then we'll be exchanging
gifts on the 6th, the day after the last day of old-
style Christmas. "Epiphany," quips D, "I always thought
they called it that because it's all over!"

-- Ordinarily I'd be filling out my fortnightly

[Theory of a Unified Jyzefield]

Employment Security forms right now. They're due
tomorrow, or rather tomorrow's the earliest they can be
mailed in to qualify for the next check. But I'll hold
off a little bit this time.

     Mother assures me Barb hasn't gone religious. I'm
all but certain she's wrong. Barb may not even know
it's happened herself. In her view the theologian whose
sermon she sent us may be primarily some kind of
transcendental mystic who identifies with this
particular deity just because it's locally sanctioned,
i.e. in certain parts of the Americas and Europe,
mostly. Mother also chides me for being "so critical"
of Barb and says Jeff and Rob just shake their heads
over the way the two of us go after each other. And
right on cue I think: oh yeah? So what's Barb saying to
them behind my back this time to make them think that?

     But the grim reality is: it's all about to become
strictly marginal. Mother and Jim Q. are at each
other's throats again (he's back on lithium because the
other stuff, though in Mother's view it improves his
disposition enormously, makes him feel lobotomized).
She may soon revert to living alone in her apartment and
this time be scarcely able to move. Then what? Death
might be a more merciful alternative. "Call in --," as
D would say ("doc of death" again). (And Barb will hold
it against me that she'll be the one more or less forced
to deal directly with most of Mother's everyday needs in
the interim, even though this is exactly the way Barb
always insisted she wanted it and in fact the way she's
more or less arranged it by choosing to live within a
mile of her.)

     -- But here it comes, the annual Christmas Eve
postmidnight reading on the grooveyard: "...When what to
my wondering eyes should appear...." Wotta voice!
Think what jazz has given the world! (And every year
when this comes on I think: had the man ever even seen
the lyrics before? I doubt it. -- And that's genius.)

     But. But -- what kind of week was it? Rain rain
rain. And more work than expected, with reporter Naomi
taking reporter Verna's grand jury for the second time

this month. Does this mean Verna is easing out? That
her new arrangement with dayscoper Doris isn't going so
well? That she's thinking she'd be better off taking
less difficult jobs which she can scope herself on the
fancy home unit which she has to pay for anyway
regardless of how much she uses it? Quite possibly yes
to all these. But no way to know for sure just yet.

I did leave Naomi a mock-official note saying the
Jyzer Ink "board of directors" had reached its decision
and the sole proprietor under its jurisdiction now
stands ready to meet all her scoping needs in the coming
year. Also said in a P.S. not to worry, D and I have
come up with a way to keep on scraping by. In truth,
though, it's mostly Naomi herself who's saving us. She
and the U's.

Living on the edge is no fun (and never mind what I
may have blithely written to the contrary in the past)
(and also never mind what this "Art Lives on Edge"
button says right here with its cartoon happy face) but
it sure does beat the alternative of going over or
falling off (the edge, that is, yes).

Rain rain rain. And it's raining again now after a
brief respite. "I'm Dreaming Of A Wet Wet Wet One."
It's loud out there. And this the first official week
of winter.

-- Funny, though, that word "edge," I've been
thinking about it all week, how I've got to get mine
back. The kind of edge that comes from tension and
surprise -- but only when you're "writing out of an
excited passion." All right, yes, I came across that
very (banal) phrase somewhere in the last few days, but
the truth is I've looked at things essentially that way
my entire writing life. Could any slogan, banal or not,
be more obviously true? Yet I needed reminding. It's
possible I was sinking into some stupid moroseness
again. Yes it is.

Silent night. Holy night. Playing now. The
traditional carol itself but in updated form, a brace of
buffoonish trombones lending it an odd yet not unseemly
dignity. Holy brasserie!

[Theory of a Unified Jyzefield]

(Another swig of Ol' Grizzlie Bite and this time
the shudder goes all the way down. Shake head like a
marimba. Screw eyeballs back in.)
     -- Where was I? Yes, ghosts. Christmases past.
Suddenly (it seems) they're everywhere, more of them now
than this jyze will ever be able to summon for a revisit
in a single sitting. And the best, not to say the most
active, of the ones haunting me in recent days come from
right around the years I'm trying to write about in the
Mentoka series. My last few Christmases at home in
Gatewood -- when I was living and going to school in
Mentoka Falls.
     The darkness of Christmas. The cruelty of life.
Well yeah. But we've always known about this --
especially the big part that's built right in -- so why
make a big deal of it if we don't have to? And thank
the gods I (for one) don't have to right now/just yet.
     Coming up on half past two on this Christmas
morning. (Sez the usual mild-mannered grooveyard jock,
who's handling the station breaks all by himself tonight
and also turning out to be an ineradicable even if
anonymous presence in these pages.)
     Several more cards arrived yesterday. One from
good old Tom T., my commute buddy. A nice surprise. I
whipped one back to him, antic camels and all. (Will
anything come of all this good cheer? Probably not.)
     "Next year," belts out the jazz tribune of this
moment, "all our troubles will be out of sight!"
     Timely stuff, absolutely. What would I do without
this station? No doubt it should get a credit on any
and all writings of mine that come out of this era.
     No Christmas tree this year. Around here who needs
one anyway? We've got scores of them growing right out
in the yard and thousands more within easy viewing
distance from any door or window in the house. But by
and large we haven't been in the mood, that's all --
meaning I haven't, since by default I'm the Christmas
impresario around here -- except for the last few hours.
And even now the voltage is not what it might be. (No
Christmas lights this year either, outdoors I mean. Or

indoors either, except for the string that's up year-round in my study window and currently inoperative because of a single bad bulb of a type apparently unobtainable anywhere within a ten-mile radius.)

 -- Reminding me: from B&B we learned Captain Brick has a long record of drug busts. So the plot thickens. And Ben filled us in on those screams that tore apart the weekend nights last summer. I was close to right in the first place: they came from that gaggle of skinheads who rented the "ranchette" to the southeast, uphill from both B&B and Brick & Jenny. Seven in all, five males. The cops were called out on them twice and finally they were busted for burglary at the bible church and dealing "dippers" (weed laced with animal trank) behind the town store. Another local story with legs which jyze overlooked because of its preoccupations elsewhere. (And the glabrous gaggle might just as easily have targeted my shed or this house.)

 The last few entries (bursts!) I've been sabotaging myself. It's been happening off and on ever since I decided to type up these ramblings and eventually go public with them. It's only natural. It's the only way I can go on having fun. And it seems to work. Call it sabotage jyze. Self-unfulfilling. I'd say it has a future. Of sorts. Because it's self-consuming also. The black hole of prose. Deeply secular for sure. (But is the black of the hole the ink or is it the absence of ink?)

 But what a way to talk at three a.m. on Christmas morning. "I'll Be Home For Christmas." Blow it my man. I'll be right here. I am. In Ol' Grizzlie Bite bad form. Looking for new ways to undermine and decompose. Yeah. But in antientropic fashion, absolutely.

 -- Admittedly I'm just about done in. But first one last item. It's Jyzer G's surprise Xmas gift for future jyzers everywhere. Yes! Which is what? Well, it's the jyze manifesto itself, but a compressed version limited to ten points on a single typed page. "The Ten Arms of the Jyzopus." More like a punch list actually. In any case: I'll be attaching it hereto as an appendix.

[Theory of a Unified Jyzefield]

Stamp this thing "Ministry of Jyze Approved."
(And to all a Grizzlie good night.)

5.

It's just about over. For many it already is.
We've listened to the new one roll across the land at a
thousand miles an hour and at this very moment they're
cheering its arrival back in the M. zone. A renowned
jazz organist is tearing away live, the chords and notes
bouncing jaggedly off walls back there and also right
here in our own toasty little corner of the outback.
In the shadow of the green heat-saving tarp
partition this is. I'm hanging out at our dining-area
table tonight. Brought in the desk lamp from my study
especially for this occasion. Also brought in the last
few swigs -- toxic for sure -- of Ol' Grizzlie Bite.
Electric wall heater blasting a foot to the left.
A shelf of memorabilia suspended maybe eight inches
above the wallward portion of the table (this setup is
way too complicated to try to describe -- and it's the
former site of the fruit bowl that D immortalized in the
watercolor now hanging in her room). The shiny blue
hippo's up there, the new ceramic "Mentoka cow," a
panda, a pair of wooden mandarin love ducks (a "D"
painted in orange on the back of one, a "G" on the
other), a large Norwegian wooden rosemaling plate (gift
from Mother), a framed photo of the super-adorable
nineteen-year-old D posing in swimsuit but capless on
the high board at a college meet (a few weeks before she
nearly killed herself banging her head on that same
board in mid-dive and retired from the sport forever),
and several small Christmas items (our entire display
for this year). And at my back the lamp burns by my
reading chair, right in front of Jhe couch where the
birthday peanut gallery held forth lo these many moons
ago. And the big glass picture window behind the chairs

183

is streaked with moisture and so is the glass door to
the deck at the far end of the room, a/k/a the "parlor"
(still). This being one of those nights when all the
moisture is inside, not outside, the glass.

Don't know why I, contempo G, am being so literal
here. Been stuck in the real too long. This must
change. -- Thrashing and stuttering to close out the
year.

(She calls from the basement. Possibly I left a
heater on down there. Or now she's saying Vinnie misses
me. -- Vinnie's the near-feral black cat we've been
inviting into the "library" on unusually cold nights
after Fred's tucked in up here. Vinnie's become my
companion during the long hours of working on "Mentoka
Dreams" structure and "Jyzeburst" proofing and renewed
(clandestine) "Jyzer" prepping. He curls up on a burlap
coffee bag at the end of the couch with one eye fixed
warily on me as I perch atop my cushions in the middle.)

What happened this year? A lucky break -- I got
RIF'd. It'll look even luckier if any of these writing
projects of mine ever amount to anything. Then I can
call it a fortunate jolt. And certainly I'll want to
find some way to do that regardless, if possible.

The second good thing: I started this new kind of
scratching and called it jyze. Called it JIRT. Called
it JIFT, for jyze in fictive time, yes: have I ever
officially noted this before? And called it JIFT/JIRT.
Became a jyze/JIFT/JIRT fanatic.

(The live jazz show is now jumping from the Mentoka
zone to our zone. Skipping right over Mountain! How
steamed we'd've been in our Mountain days!)

Was there a third good thing? D and I managed to
survive with our couplehood intact. D herself survived
another health scare. Mother survived. In fact, as far
as I'm aware, and D too, everyone else we personally
knew at the start of the year has survived the year.

And bad things. Loss of much of our only assured
source of income, that's got to be bad. New intimations
of mortality in several close-in realms. New cracks in
the couplehood. Imminent loss of this house and land

(and shed!). Delay of my major writing project at the worst possible time. Worrisome new tensions arising between me and sister Barb. Beginning of a new era of heightened reclusion (which has its good side too).

    -- After staying up all day readying a trio of blank 224-page jyzebooks for next year (tattooing the inside front covers with "Made in USA" and "Artistic Malfunction" and all that other good stuff: almost as if I've finally fully morphed into fictive narrator G of "Jyzer") -- after that, I say, I trudged down to the driveway mailbox at three p.m. and found two envelopes, each enclosing a check, one from the scope firm and one from ES. So we're in business subsistence-wise for two more weeks. In fact the two checks combined total $872, which is only about $80 less than what my standard check from the firm for the same pay period used to be. But most of the time they'll add up to significantly less -- somewhere between $700 and $800. And that's before taxes; the regular check was after. And the next set will be only slightly above $600 pretax because I won't have worked at all during the two holiday weeks (unless something changes next week, which is far from likely).

    Can we keep on keeping on? That's the crucial question. But that's for next time and thereafter, not now. I'm trying to save all future-oriented matters for the first entry of the year jyze two.

    I did sit down and force myself to read through a weekly USAn news magazine's end-of-year issue. Truly a dismaying piece of work. In the past few years the mainstream media have drifted so far rightward they're almost unrecognizable. Just like the country itself, some might say, but no, I don't believe that. Election results and other surface disturbances are misleading. (And may the gods help us if they're not. -- Not that we as a nation deserve the gods' help, or at least not to the degree just about any other nation does, given what we, the reigning self-appointed master of them all, have done and are doing and no doubt will continue doing just as long as we can get away with it, and to as many

of those nations as possible and to the planet as a
whole in order to maintain our position as ruler of --
the planet as a whole, yes. Or is it the multiverse
now? -- But then why shouldn't the gods be good to
everyone, us included? -- But I suppose they'd be more
inclined to be that way if we were to change some of our
more egregious behavior first.)

Preach! Preach! What, you some kind of woo-woo
radic-prog? Well maybe, but here I'm just being
neoprag. Just hoping for some redemptive moves before
it's too late. But let's face it, even if those took
place, this nation's long-term prospects, along with
those of most if not all the others -- but in our case
far more so -- would still be very, very poor.

-- And what's good? What's really good is that
things still mean something on the personal level, or at
least seem to. And that by itself is enough, for now.
For tonight. For this whole week maybe. (Testify!)

-- The New Year keeps rolling our way. A local
vocalist who's made good on the national scene is at the
radio mic. Some dynamite sax player behind her. Is
that -- and I think of a certain name which of course
the jyze rules say I can't mention. (But I'm starting
to wonder if maybe I know a little more than I thought I
did about jazz.) (Give the jyzer some! -- And do it on
faith alone! -- As if there were any other choice.)

Now considering -- yes, a couple of new wrinkles in
my work situation. For one, I discovered Jyzer Ink has
become "Vendor 173." That's how the paper file
containing all material relating to my current work for
the firm is labeled. For another, they've recently made
up a computer file called, according to a handwritten
list, "Employment Security Claims," but despite an
extensive search I've been unable to locate it in their
system. Maybe they know more about my status with ES
than I've been thinking. I'll be checking further into
all this -- but never mind, that's future too.

Past. The year jyze one. What about it? Inspire
us all, goddamn it! Fire us up!

Well, okay, how about this:

[Theory of a Unified Jyzefield]

A THUNDERBOLT RIGHT THIS INSTANT
UNIFIES THE JYZEFIELD.

    Yes!
    -- In theory it ought to work, JIRT and JIFT
perking along in parallel and J. Ink paying the bills.
In practice -- well, we'll see. The unending test.
(Could be that's why it's called theory.) (Could also
be I'd temperamentally prefer a fractured jyzefield.
-- Or call it Jyze 3.0 with a triple mope dimension.)
    (Now she's padding around in the kitchen. Started
to talk but then realized the jyzer's hard at it on the
other side of the green tarp. And indeed he is, grim
and begrizzled and be-Grizzlied, hand shading eyes and
propping up furrowed brow. This sorry apparition
surreally distorted by the condensation-streaked window;
and in the same reflection, at least from his angle and
not failing to include patchy memory augmentations, the
ghostly old peanut gallery of last August seems to be
rolling its eyes and twisting itself into pretzel-faces
of mirth. -- Tough jyze room here again tonight, yeah.)
    How long until midnight anyway? At which point one
really ought to lay this J-book down. Though it would
be easy to come up with a rationale for continuing late
into the night (as indeed earlier avatars of this G
right here have done with urjyze and protojyze on many
another New Year's Eve) -- although it would be easy to
do that, I say, I don't think I should do it on this
particular night. No. Because I've got something
different here. Up in the shed I was thinking just that
-- something different, I've saved myself, or
something's saved me, and now I'll have a new volume to
put at the end of the shelf. And this is good. This is
the best. This when I get right down to it is the best
of all, for this year and probably any year.
    -- The end of which annum, i.e. this one, is very
nearly upon us, as shown by growing excitement coming
from the radio. And meanwhile, with splendid timing,
here's the last page. The last time I'll ever meet up

with the notes. In the future -- but no. The future
will explain itself in next year's jyze -- will you ever
get that straight you jyzonic blockhead? (Chopping off
the future like this can leave you stumping around in
gorky confusion. It's downright unnatural.)
So why not try some slashes at the back too?

/////////DDD////
///// J ///// GGG ///// YEE-HA! /////

(Ooh, how the jyzer's been wanting to do that! -- Just
wish he'd/I'd thought of firing up old No. 3 for the
task of scratching-slashing-splashing out the whole
final entry. But it's way too late for that now.)
-- And the noisemakers are sounding and the
announcer is calling out "One minute, one minute!" and
the applause is very loud and the countdown chant is
picking up.
So this is it, year filled. To the extent I, this
G, this jyzerperson, am able. Or to jyze limits anyway,
and factoring in the late start.
Fifteen, fourteen, thirteen...five, four, three...
Bedlam!
"Should all ajyzance be forgot...."
(Oooh the schmaltz of this moment. -- So where'd
that Mel Bear go? Big traditional slobbery New Year's
kiss coming atcha. Or she might think the jyzer's too
Grizzlied-up for that. But yes we need to be getting
our groove back on and I mean right now.)

END

APPENDIX

The Ten Arms of the Jyzopus

1. Make each entry the same preset target
    length (say ten pages), with min/max
    limits (say eight, twelve pages);
2. Observe a preset interval (jyzeweek)
    between entries, preferably an even
    number of days so that jyzeday will
    always fall in cyclical fashion on a
    different day of the week ("On the
    eighth day he/she jyzed");
3. Fill a jyzebook to the last page in a
    certain preset period (say four months),
    with any failures to meet (1) and (2)
    above compensated for in order to meet
    (3) (i.e., if short one page one entry,
    add an extra for the next entry, etc.);
4. At some point in each entry describe the
    setting of that entry ("where it's
    coming from");
5. Always choose for each entry (if
    possible) a setting different from all
    previous settings in the same volume;
6. Give each entry a "hook" in the larger
    world (i.e., events, news, politics);
7. Advance the jyzer's personal narrative
    in each entry (i.e., what's happened
    to him/her since the previous entry);
8. Maintain awareness in each entry of
    overarching story, pace and developing
    themes and characters for the jyzeyear
    as a whole, fictional novel fashion;
9. Avoid use of brand names, personal names
    (except for those of acquaintances, and
    then first names and initials only), and
    place names (except for those of
    countries and world regions) (but names
    and places from fiction are okay);
10. Inflect all the above through gnarly
    jyzer self: mood, conflicts, temper,
    hopes, gripes, dreams, unconscious.
    (Poke that hurt! Twang those tensions!)
    (over)

(Not that the jyzopus needs even a single one of
these arms to lean on. Chop off as many as you like and
you can keep on jyzing regardless. And sooner or later
the arms will grow back anyway, though they might not be
recognizable at first or ever.)

9 780099 641731